To young Elizabeth Mawes and Robert Linnly, runaway indentured servants, Easton Township means hope after a long and terrifying journey northward. There they will find jobs, security, and at last freedom. But as they approach the end of their journey, a new struggle awaits them—a struggle upon which Robert's future and Elizabeth's life depend.

Continuing the story begun in his highly acclaimed *Night Journeys*, Avi has once again created a compelling historical novel with depth, suspense, and fast-paced adventure.

Also by Avi

Things that Sometimes Happen
Snail Tail
No More Magic
Captain Grey
Emily Upham's Revenge
Night Journeys

Encounter at Easton

AVI

Pantheon Books

Library of Congress Cataloging in Publication Data
Avi, 1937– Encounter at Easton.
Summary: The doomed flight of two young indentured
servants from their unkind master brings together an
unlikely assortment of people in a mid-18th-century
Pennsylvania town. [1. Indentured servants—Fiction.
2. Runaways—Fiction. 3. Pennsylvania—Fiction]
I. Title. PZ7.A953En [Fic] 79–9439
ISBN 0–394–84342–8 ISBN 0–394–94342–2 lib. bdg.

To Phoebe

ENCOUNTER AT EASTON

Lord Bowden
Bowden House
Bristol,
England

My Lord:

It has come to my attention that you desire information concerning Elizabeth Mawes and Robert Linnly, the young persons transported to America from England some years back, being no more than common felons.

Among papers in the Easton Courthouse I came upon the recorded Testimony of three men and a boy, taken down as they spoke at some sort of hearing in the spring of 1768.

I have copied out their words, placing each testimony in order that it might read as a tale.

It is not, My Lord, a pretty story. I only beg that once begun you continue till the end.

Trusting my efforts will meet with your approval, I remain, Sir,

your most humble servant, and etc . . .

J. Dankers
Recorder

Testimony of Nathaniel Hill, of Trenton

I understand that I, Nathaniel Hill have been accused of wishing to do the girl harm. It is not true, simply not true. In the first place, though I am a person of reduced means, I *am* a gentleman. I never knew her, and I never wanted to know her. It was by a mere coincidence that I became entangled. In short, it was nothing more than an encounter at Easton. You may be certain it was a most unpleasant encounter for me.

So, to begin with, on my word of honor as a gentleman, what you have heard is untrue.

If I have a fault—and who amongst us does not have at least one fault?—it is that I am too trusting. If you were to tell me a thing was so, I would be obliged to believe you. It is my nature. This trouble in which I find myself comes from—what shall I say?—from putting too much faith in others, especially those who are my inferiors.

Now, as to what happened: It was April of this year, 1768, the end of the harsh winter, a restless time in this miserable town known as Trenton. I was taking my ease at the only decent tavern thereabouts, the George Three, enjoying a small refreshment while playing a hand of cards, when Mr. R. entered.

It does not matter here who Mr. R. is, or was, or will be. He is merely cause, not effect. What needs more to be said, save that he is my inferior? Let it also be admitted that from time to time we played cards. A gentleman's profession, a gentleman's profession.

It so happened that I owed this Mr. R. a sum of money, a mere twelve pounds. Not, as you can see, a great amount. I was aware of my obligation and meant to pay him in good time. Not once before had this Mr. R. pressed me about it.

That night, however, he came into the tavern, presumed to approach me, and begged leave to speak. When free of my game I joined him, though I could see at once it bode ill. What ailed him I do not know, nor did I ever learn. I do not meddle in other people's affairs.

He came to his point after some hesitation.

"I am in need of the money you owe me," said he, obviously embarrassed, though it did nothing to tie his tongue.

"I intend to pay," I reassured him, pointing out that at the moment he found me a bit low.

"I must have it at once," he pleaded.

"Must you?" I said. "How inconvenient. I do not have it to give."

He was in a fair sweat. I daresay he was nervous, since I have something of a fierce reputation.

"I am sorry to be asking," he whispered, "but I am truly in great need."

I recall taking out my double-barreled pistol at this point, placing it on the table, and beginning to clean it. It is a habit I have. "What if I cannot give it to you?" I asked with a politeness which his station did not deserve.

"Then I am a ruined man!" says he.

"What is that to me?" I said.

He grew red in the face and stood all atremble. I could even see the teary bilge about his eyes. "Please, sir," he said. "If I do not have the money within the month, I shall be positively ruined!"

What could I do? Whatever his paltry reasons, the man was frantic, and I have a rule that suggests it is unwise to squeeze a frantic man. Besides, all in all, no matter what you may hear, I have a soft heart. I told him I would get his beastly money for him. The wretch all but kissed my hands. When I dismissed him, he positively fled.

But I had done it. Bad enough to owe such a rascal a penny. Worse, I had actually promised to pay him within the month. I was a fool—I own it—and it comes of being too soft.

What, then, was I to do? I made some inquiries

and looked to such resources as I had; but I found nothing, nothing at all. What with other demands being put upon me I was beginning to think I might have to become a gentleman of the road. Happily, fortune—or what I took to be fortune—caught me up.

{ 2 }

Testimony of Mr. John Tolivar, Gentleman of Trenton

I am John Tolivar, Esquire. Now you must attend to what I say carefully, for I have no intention of spending any more of my valuable time on this sordid affair. Rest perfectly assured that what happened had nothing to do with me. Obviously, it was entirely due to the blundering of a host of individuals, most of whom I do not know. I trust I never shall.

The truth of the matter is, this country is plagued by bunglers, men who have more excuses to drop things than they have fingers to hold. There is no respect for such persons as myself, or, for that matter, the law.

I reside in Trenton, where I own considerable property. Labor being scarce, I make it my business to buy up contract labor from England. In doing so one cannot be choosy, and thus last fall I purchased two transported felons, young ones, a boy and a girl. No relation. Their names: Elizabeth Mawes and Robert Linnly. They were, as I say, transported felons, and the girl was branded on the thumb for the malefactor she was.

To come to the point: The two were not content to be spared the gallows, not content with a free voyage from England, not content with the promise of freedom at the age of twenty-one. No! They took it upon themselves to run off, to escape. No doubt some unscrupulous persons dazzled them with fair dreams of freedom.

Mind, what I say now I did not know then: They headed northward, for Easton. And why Easton? Because Easton is in Pennsylvania, the fastest way out of Jersey Colony and is, moreover, populated by a people notoriously soft. Mind, the two felons dared not go to Philadelphia. Unattached children are quickly caught there.

In contrast, Easton is as far away as one can get in Pennsylvania by road. Indeed, it is on the edge of the wilderness. They say labor is scarce there, work can be found, and the devil only minds where a person is from. I suppose this Elizabeth Mawes and Robert Linnly heard these rumors, and so they set their course.

As soon as I learned of their escape I hurried up and down both sides of the Delaware River—not knowing then where the two were headed—proclaiming a reward for their capture. The reward was high enough to attract interest.

When I came back that first night I paused to rest at the George Three. While there, I was approached by a Mr. Nathaniel Hill. Please note that he approached me; I did not approach him.

I do not know this Mr. Hill other than by reputation. Though he gives himself the style of a gentleman, he is better known as bully and rascal. More often than not he spends his time doing things for people they prefer not doing for themselves.

When he accosted me, it was to ask for possible employment. It was only natural that I informed him that I had that day lost two servants. I mentioned the reward. This tickled his ears so much that he offered to fetch them back for me if I gave him fifty pounds.

Fifty pounds, by God! That is the sort of rascal he is. I told him to go hang himself. I would not be toyed with.

On the second day after the escape I was pleased to learn that the boy, Robert Linnly, had been caught up north, by Coryell's Ferry. The girl was yet free, but the searchers fully expected her to be found.

This news set my mind very much at rest, and I went back to the George Three. Once again Mr. Hill approached me, this time offering to do the job for thirty pounds. Laughing, I had the pleasure of informing him that the boy had been taken and that the capture of the girl was expected momentarily.

He shrugged, and bothered me no more.

On the third day, however, I received intelligence that the girl had still not been found. Further, I was given to understand that she was presumably well on her way toward Easton. I did two things: I made the reward higher, and I summoned Mr. Hill.

I provided him with the truth as I knew it then: that the boy was caught but that the girl was still at large, either close to or in Easton. I offered him fifteen pounds if he were to bring Elizabeth Mawes back, five pounds if he went to search for her and met with no success.

He accepted instantly.

I provided Mr. Hill with Elizabeth Mawes' contract papers, proving her to be a runaway. I informed him that all he needed to do, once he found her, was to show the papers to the local constable. That done, he would have the right to claim the girl and bring her back to me.

Further, I provided Mr. Hill with a description of the girl, reminding him that she was a transported felon and bore an M-shaped brand on her right thumb. Moreover, I gave him the loan of a horse and money for expenses. He could hardly fail.

And indeed, he made a great point of assuring me it was no more to him than a little adventure, an excuse to get out of Trenton after a sodden winter. He "could use the exercise" were his exact words. In short, it was to be a holiday for him.

He set off that night.

You may well imagine, then, my extraordinary

annoyance the very next morning when one of my men returned from Coryell's Ferry, whence he had gone to bring back the boy, Robert Linnly. Now my man reported that the boy was again free. Once more he had escaped!

How was this done? You may well ask. As I subsequently learned, the constable at Coryell's Ferry—the devil take him—the one who was holding the escaped boy, had bungled. It seems that someone in this constable's family had taken pity on Robert Linnly and had let him go. Not only was the runaway let go, but he was provided a horse. Imagine! A runaway was given a horse! And indeed, as I was later to learn, Robert Linnly *did* rejoin Elizabeth Mawes and *together* they did go to Easton.

Alas, it was too late to send word of this horrendous development to Mr. Hill. Remember, he had gone off thinking the girl was *alone*. No doubt this in part explains what occurred.

As for myself, I knew no more until I received word of the events in Easton. But by then, of course, it was too late.

{ 3 }

Testimony of the Boy, Robert Linnly

My name is Robert Linnly. I will tell you what happened to Elizabeth.

When I awoke that morning—it was three days since we had left Trenton—I was sitting behind Elizabeth atop the mare. We were slowly going up a hill, the top of which was a clearing. There the horse came to a stop.

"Easton," said Elizabeth.

The road we had followed had been closed in by trees. But at the top of the hill, before the road turned down, there was an open view. From it we could see where the Lehigh River joined the Delaware.

On the far side of the river sat Easton, some sixty buildings rising from the morning's low mist. They seemed to guard the forest, which went endlessly beyond. Most of the houses were wood, though a few were brick.

But it is about Elizabeth that I need to tell. When we had crossed the Delaware River after making our escape—we crossed by Coryell's Ferry—we became separated. I was caught, but I managed to escape and find Elizabeth again. Only when I rejoined her did I learn that her left arm had been hurt when she had crossed the river. What is more, so intent was I on our getting away that I had paid little mind to it. Besides, the covering bandage meant I never saw the wound or knew how bad it truly was.

How different all might have been if I had known otherwise!

I must describe for you what Elizabeth was like that day we came to Easton. For her twelve years of age she was not very big. I am somewhat younger than she but was close to her in size. Her skirt was too large for her, and on her long hair she wore no bonnet. As she sat astride the mare her left hand rested in her lap while her right held the bridle. It was on her right hand that she had been branded.

When she told me Easton lay before us, I leaned out from the horse and looked in the direction she pointed.

"It's not very big," I said, disappointed.

"You're always dreaming things better," she said. She spoke almost gaily, for she was one who liked to tease. "It's only sleep I need."

"I didn't mean to sleep so long," I said, feeling guilty because I had dozed so much during the night. "The horse plods so."

"It doesn't matter," she said, her voice losing its lightness. "We're here."

"Do you think we can find work?" I asked. I always questioned her about such things, feeling that she knew much more than I.

"We shall have to," she answered with a sudden yawn. "I'm hungry enough."

"And tired too," I added.

For a few moments we rested, content to look at the two rivers.

"We shan't go across there," she said, pointing at the waterfall where the two rivers joined. "They are sure to have a ferry upriver."

"We will have to pay to cross on the ferry," I said, worried, for we had no coin at all.

When she said nothing to this, I looked at her more closely. Only then did I truly see how weary she was.

"I'd rather sleep before we go over," she said.

"Is it your arm?" I suddenly asked, for I had touched her arm and she had jerked it away.

She shrugged her shoulders, as if it did not matter.

"We may have been followed," I said. "So we'll be safer in town. If we don't find work right away, Bet, we can sell the horse. That will keep us for awhile."

"We haven't been followed," she said matter-of-factly. "They'd have caught us by now if we had been."

"We'll get across some way," I said. "And when we do, we can turn off the road and hide in the woods if you like. Sleep, if that's your fancy. I think it is. I can go to town alone, find work, gain a day's wage, and bring back food. Won't that be fine for a day's doings?" I remember saying all this just as if it would happen that easily.

She shook her head. "No, don't go without me."

I thought to say we might have no choice in the matter. Instead, I only urged that we go on a little farther. She agreed, and slowly the horse began to move once more, down the crest of the hill, up along the Lehigh River.

After we had traveled for about a mile beyond the hill, Elizabeth abruptly made the horse stop. "I can not go any farther," she announced. "I am too tired."

I got down from the horse right away. Telling Bet to just hold on, I took the reins and guided the mare into the bushes. After some twenty or thirty feet, we came to an enclosed place. Stopping, I held up my arms to lift her down. As I did, I looked into her face and what I saw upset me. She was very pale, her eyes were dull, and her lips, tightly shut, seemed almost bloodless.

"You can sleep here," I told her, tramping down the tall grass with my bare feet. It was a place that I thought might be warmed by the sun.

Hardly waiting for me to say more, she took the spot and lay down. "I shan't sleep long," she murmured, her eyes already closed.

For a long time I just stood there, wishing there was something with which to cover her. In spite of the sun's rays, the morning was still cool. But there was nothing, and so I turned instead to see where we were.

It was a well-protected place, and since we had met no one during the hours of our flight along the Delaware River, I felt secure. Still, just to be certain, I went out on the road again to look into the bushes where Elizabeth lay and the horse stood. To my eyes they were perfectly hidden. Relieved, I went back to them and sat across from Elizabeth and waited.

As more and more time went by, I became impatient. I began to feel the need to do something, anything. We were so close to our goal, Easton, and yet here we remained. I waited as long as I could, and then decided—out of my impatience—to do a small thing. It *was* a small thing. But, as you shall see, the consequence was great.

My decision was this: I would go down the road and investigate the ferry. After that I would come back. That was all I decided, but having made at least one decision, I felt very much better. It was, after all, something to do.

Untying the horse, I returned once more to the

road and there climbed up on the mare's back. Even then, I remember feeling unsure whether to go or not. But what harm could come to Elizabeth in so short a time? I asked myself. Oh, how I wish now that I had stayed where I was!

{4}

Testimony of Robert Linnly,
continued

I rode easily down the road. I was striving to be hopeful, just as I had tried to put down any worry about leaving Elizabeth alone. The brightening sun felt warm, and that helped. After all, the two of us had come so far that it was hard to think anything wrong could lay before us. As far as I was concerned, we had only to move beyond the river and everything bad would be left behind. My spirits did rise.

The road continued for about half a mile, then turned down and to the right, toward the river, and—or so I hoped—toward a ferry. Soon I saw the river at the end of an avenue of trees.

Once certain of my bearings, I stopped, for this was as far as I had planned to come. Seeing nothing to trouble me, however, I decided to be sure there really was a ferry. I thought too that I might be able to find out what the toll was and bargain for a crossing. I reached the river's edge in a few moments. Once there, I got off the horse and let her graze.

The Lehigh River is not nearly as wide as the Delaware. Also, the Lehigh is shallow, though here and there it seemed deep. In the morning sun it looked very bright, running so freely that I thought there would be nothing better than to *be* a river. A silly, foolish thought, but it tells how I was thinking.

There was no question but that I had reached a ferry landing. From an overhanging tree two metal bars hung close together, and I guessed that you struck one bar against the other when you wanted the boat to come. Looking across and slightly downstream, I thought I spied the ferry; it was no more than a large flat-bottomed boat. But there was no sign at the landing to tell me how much a crossing would cost.

I was standing there, just gazing out on the water, when I was startled by a sound behind me. Turning quickly, I saw that a man had ridden up on horseback. To my great relief it was nobody I recognized. I saw, too, that while he was dressed in good clothes, he was muddy and unkempt. His hat was dusty, his once white stockings hung limp, and his hair was in disarray.

He gave me a swift look, but I felt he had no

particular interest in me. I was not frightened of him, though I will admit I wondered if, in passing down the road, he had seen Elizabeth.

"Morning!" he addressed me.

I returned the greeting.

"Is this the ferry landing?" he asked. He said this in a friendly enough fashion, as though asking someone who lived nearby.

"I think so," I replied, feeling more relaxed now.

"Not certain?" he said.

"I'm not from hereabouts," I answered, and immediately was sorry to have said so. Indeed, for a moment I grew fearful.

But he turned to stare across the river. "Traveling alone?" he wanted to know.

"Yes," I said.

Shifting on his horse, he looked at me again. "But you are going to Easton?"

I nodded.

"Where are you from?" he inquired.

"Philadelphia," I said hastily.

"A long way."

"I've a relation in Easton, an uncle," I said, trying to return his steady look as I struggled to think what to say. "I'll stay with him. He says work can be found in Easton."

"Ah," he said, laughing. "You can find work anywhere. The trick is to get along *without* finding it!"

"Are you from Easton?" I asked.

"No," he said, "I'm just going there myself."

"Then you don't know how much it costs to cross?"

"No more than a few pennies," he suggested. Suddenly he grinned. "Is that more than you have?"

"Oh, no sir," I lied. "I have it. But I shan't be going over quite yet."

"Why is that?"

"I mean to have my breakfast first," I managed. Then, fearful that I had already spoken too much, I climbed back on the mare and turned her about.

"What's your name?" the man asked.

I gave him the first name I could think of, "Peter York."

"Master York," he said easily, "if your relation has not found you employment, you yet might wish to see me again. I intend to stay in Easton for a short time and will need a boy like you, someone to care for my horse and run such errands as I might have. Two shillings the week, which is too high, I warrant, but it's what I offer. Mind, it won't be for long, for I've no intention of staying."

I felt sudden excitement at being so lucky as to have found work. "Do you mean it?" I asked, rejoicing that we would not have to sell the horse.

"If I said it, I mean it," the man assured me.

"I would like to," I told him, already sorry I had invented the story of a relation. "I'll see what my uncle says. I don't think he'll object."

"Not for what I've offered, he won't. Now then,

my name is Nathaniel Hill," he informed me. "I'll lodge at the first decent inn I come to at Easton—if there is a decent place. You'll have to search me out. Mind, I shan't wait on you long, but I'd prefer not to hunt about for someone else."

"Yes, sir," I replied eagerly.

"Good," he returned. "Make sure you come!"

With that, he reached up to the metal bars and beat one against the other. As he did so, I turned my horse away and came from the river, greatly pleased with myself and my good fortune.

I hurried back to Elizabeth, bursting to tell her my news, only to find her just as I had left her, fast asleep. Full of excitement at my splendid luck, I waited impatiently for her to awaken.

{ 5 }

Testimony of Nathaniel Hill,
continued

When I took my leave of Mr. Tolivar in Trenton, his money and papers in my saddlebags, his horse beneath me, I proceeded north along the river. I took my time in leaving, for it is not my way to hurry. I even took pains to find Mr. R., informing him that relief was on the way and that he need not blow out his brains quite yet. It was thus dark when I left, and such moonlight as there was only allowed me to go at a modest rate.

All the same, I did push the horse—not a very good mount, by the by—and we traveled all night. It was early morning before I reached the crest of the hill from which I saw Easton for the first time.

I must admit I had thought it merely a settlement, and so my first view of the town's many dwellings came as something of a surprise. Then and there I was forced to alter my plans.

If Easton had been a tiny community, I could

simply have gone around making the necessary inquiries, then left, with or without the girl. But as it was much larger, I saw that not only would it take a systematic search but it would unfortunately require some sort of stay for me to be sure—if I ever could be sure—that the girl was there.

Not being one to languish over disappointments, I merely accepted these conclusions and continued down the road—such as it was—until I reached a ferry landing. I discovered I was not the only one waiting to cross; a boy was also there.

He was a young boy—I fancied no more than eleven or twelve. He had a pale face and rather dull features, though his eyes were lively enough. Such clothing as he wore was poor—he wore no boots or shoes—but, all in all, there seemed not the least thing extraordinary about him.

We exchanged the normal pleasantries, during which time he informed me he had just arrived from Philadelphia and was on his way to Easton where he had a relation. He also told me his name was Peter York.

Now I shall have to admit that there was a nervousness about him that puzzled me at first, but I put it down to the fact that he was no more than a scamp, whereas I was a gentleman.

It so happened that as we talked he mentioned he was searching for employment. It came to my mind that since I would be staying in Easton for a while, upon Mr. Tolivar's bill, I had need of a boy to clean my boots, mind my horse, and run errands. In short, I thought I could save myself trouble—which is a thing I prefer to do—by engaging him as my servant on the spot.

No sooner thought than said. He brightened at once. Whatever nervousness he had fell away, and he gave me every reason to believe he would accept my offer of service at high pay for a few days. I was quite satisfied.

When he informed me that he was not yet about to cross the river, I provided him with my name and extracted a promise from him to meet me at the earliest possible time. This done, he bade me good-bye and took himself off.

I banged the bars and stood waiting for the ferry. While standing there, my thoughts returned to how I might proceed in search of the girl.

As a person inevitably does when he goes any-where in too much haste—a thing I detest—I naturally remembered things I might have done to better organize myself. What I most regretted was not having interviewed the second runaway, the boy who had been caught, in order to gain information about the girl.

To be honest—a thing I am out of force of habit—I confess that it did cross my mind that the very boy to whom I had just spoken might have been that same runaway. But I hastily reassured myself as to the impossibility of such a thing, recalling that I had been told by Mr. Tolivar himself that the boy had been captured. In any case this lad had a horse, and he was traveling alone and not with a girl. So you see, there was not the slightest reason to doubt him at his word. I have—you can see this by now, I'm sure—a trusting, open nature.

In short, I quickly dismissed such idle speculations. The ferryman, polling his boat, approached the shore and hailed me.

"Just you and the horse?" he cried.

"Aye!"

"Thought there was another!"

"Not coming yet," I called out.

"Be twopence to cross," the ferryman informed me.

When I told him I had ready money, he quickly pushed his boat to the landing. I led my horse onto the boat as soon as the ferry reached the shore. No sooner did I do that than the rascal demanded his fee. Only when I paid him off did he order me to steady my horse while he pushed us out on the river. All in all, he was a clumsy fellow.

He was an old man, white-haired, with powerful if stooped shoulders. He bent to his work but, no doubt attracted by my bearing, kept looking at me with curiosity. It occurred to me that he might well provide useful information.

"Did you bring a young girl across last night, or during the two days previous?" I asked him.

The man was nothing less than a gossip. "I might have," he informed me. "A good number go across

28

now that the weather has bettered. What did she look like?"

I described her as best I could from the description given to me by Mr. Tolivar.

"Can't truly say," the man admitted. "I might and then again, I might not. I took no such girl alone, that much I'll tell you."

Acknowledging that she might have come with a party of others, I saw that further talk was useless. Instead, I put to him questions about Easton, seeking the name of a decent inn as well as other information.

The old man had a ready tongue for everything.

As we went over I looked into the expanse of woodlands that lay on both sides of the river. "Are those areas settled at all?" I asked.

"Not the southern side where you've just come from," he said. "Least, not till you get to the Durham area. And," he continued, "as far as I know, the only one who lives that way—he waved vaguely toward the western highlands on the northern bank of the river—is the one they call Moll."

"Moll?"

"That's what they call her," said the man, grinning toothlessly. "Don't know her real name. No one does."

Gossip that he was, though I showed no interest, he continued with a shake of his head. "Woman gone mad is the truth of it. I don't see none of her even though she does live there. Mind, I don't want to see her," he said, spitting into the river. "No, if it's decent land you want, you go t'other side of Easton. Too many hills to the west. Yes, you'd have to be mad to live there."

He then proceeded to give far more advice than I would have wanted even if I had been truly interested. Nothing would stop him but that we reached the other side.

Once on the Easton shore of the river I followed the old man's directions and soon reached the town itself.

Though not as small as I thought it to be, it was not particularly civilized either. Considerable activity was centered on a muddy market street with homes and shops in a thick and filthy cluster.

In town I proceeded slowly, paying attention to any girls I saw, thinking they might be Elizabeth Mawes. Once, perhaps twice, I felt obliged to peer for a closer look, but it came to naught.

Even so, I deliberately passed the town's only inn, the place where I was fated to stay, and traversed the full length of the town. Then back again I came through side streets and byways, so as to gain a better sense of the place, as well as to continue my search.

When I had completed these general observations, and feeling the natural fatigue of my journey, I repaired to the inn. There I secured my lodging. But such was the crudeness of the place that I had to stable my horse and attend to her. I felt greatly relieved that I had the good sense to hire a boy.

I went to my room, put my saddlebags aside, and quite naturally settled down for some well-earned sleep. My last thought before I slept was that Mr. Tolivar was going to get his money's worth.

Testimony of Robert Linnly,
continued

Elizabeth kept on sleeping. I tried
to sleep myself, just to pass the time, but I had slept
so much during the night that I was not tired.
Besides, I was increasingly hungry. A few times I
looked for berries, or anything to eat, but I found
nothing.

Impatient to move on, I kept wanting to waken
Elizabeth. The longer I waited, the more determined I was to take the man's offer of work, but I
was worried that if I didn't do so quickly, he would
get someone else. Still, knowing how tired Elizabeth
had been, I did not disturb her.

As the day wore on, a new worry came. Elizabeth
had begun to move about restlessly in her sleep.
From time to time she seemed to speak, but I could
not understand her words.

"Are you all right?" I asked more than once while
kneeling by her side.

But, instead of replying, she only slept.

I placed my hand against her brow. It felt hot, unnaturally hot. Only then did I begin to understand that she might be ill.

Hastily I went down to the river. There, I soaked my shirt in the cold water and ran back with it to wipe her face, thinking to rouse her.

I called to her, and though I thought she heard me, she said nothing in reply. My uneasiness growing, I rolled her over so that I could look more closely at the dirty and torn bandage wrapped about her hurt arm.

As soon as I removed the bandage and saw the wound, my fears grew. The wound was not bleeding but it was edged with a pulpy whiteness, the flesh around it swollen and red. I know nothing of sickness or doctoring, but I could see well enough that it was unnatural.

"Bet!" I called, fairly shouting, wanting to wake her up. Her eyes opened and she looked at me, but I could tell that she did not really see me. She had become feverish.

I didn't know what to do. The only thing I could think of was that I had to find someone, an adult, to help. Naturally I thought of the man who had offered me the job, the man I had met at the ferry landing—Mr. Hill. He, I hoped, would lend assistance. I wished I had accepted his offer of a job immediately instead of having been so cautious. In any case, he was the only person in Easton I knew. I decided to go to him.

"Elizabeth!" I cried anew, taking her right hand, trying to pull her. "You must get up. We have to get to Easton."

She only murmured something I could not understand.

The more helpless she seemed, the more frantic I grew. When at last I did get her to stand, it was as if she were half asleep. Her eyes were almost shut, her face very white, her mouth partly open. If I had not held her, she would have fallen.

"We are going to Easton," I said into her ear, feeling the heat of her on my lips. I led her toward the horse. "Get on her back," I pleaded. "You must do it. You're not well."

She tried to do as I told her, but I had to guide her every step. And even after I placed her on the mare, she slumped so, I thought she would fall off at any moment.

"We're going to the river, Elizabeth," I told her, talking to myself as much as to her. "Can you understand me?" I kept asking. "Please answer."

I thought she nodded, but I could not be sure.

I walked at the horse's side, from time to time reaching up to steady her. As we went down the road I had taken earlier, I began to talk again. I knew she could not understand me, but it made me feel better to hear my own voice.

"It's not far, Bet," I kept saying. "The ferry will be cooler. And I've found work. It will give us money so that we won't have to sell the horse.

Perhaps Mr. Hill—he's the man who offered me work—will help you. I know he'll at least find a doctor, someone to look after you. You'll get better, Bet, I know you will. It's just a little farther now. We're almost there."

Once at the ferry landing I again soaked my shirt, climbed on the horse's back, and bathed her face. Even while she was riding she seemed to have fallen into a still deeper sleep. I was now truly alarmed.

I clanged the metal bars loudly to hail the ferry. At last I saw the boat move and start to come. But the ferryman pulled up offshore.

"Just you two and the horse?" he cried out.

"Yes, sir, please," I answered, wishing the boat would come closer so that we could get on.

"What's the matter with her?" he called out, pointing to Bet.

"She's sickly, sir. Please hurry."

"It'll cost you fourpence," he said, refusing to come closer. "Do you have it?"

"No, I don't," I shouted. "But we must get to Easton."

The ferryman shook his head. "I'll take you for the money," he cried back. "But I don't carry you nor anyone else without the toll."

"She's ill!" I yelled.

"Then go up river to the fording place. That's free for the taking, and you can walk across. It's not more than three miles. You'll find an oak leaning out—you can't miss it." Saying no more, he poled

35

his boat and began to push his way back to the other side.

There was nothing else I could do. I turned the mare about, glad at least that we had the horse.

"We have to go up river, Bet," I said, though I was still not sure that she heard me. "We'll go as quickly as we can. We'll get to Easton. It won't take long."

I led the horse back up the embankment only to find that the road on which we'd come did not continue west, but ended at the landing. There was not even a path. To get to where we could ford the river, we would have to ride along the water's edge.

Down we came again, after which I climbed up on the horse to sit behind Elizabeth. Putting one arm around her and one hand to the bridle, I urged the mare to move through the shallow water. She did move, but cautiously. I wanted to hurry but I dared not, lest the horse slip or stumble. So slowly did we go that it took perhaps an hour before I saw the leaning oak that the ferryman had said marked the fording point.

"There, you see!" I called to Bet, taking some comfort in the discovery. "Now we'll get to Easton. Mr. Hill will help us. I know he will!"

Before we moved across, I stopped to look about. On either side the forest grew to all but the water's edge, and then it rose on both sides up on the hills. We stood at the bottom of a valley.

The river there seemed much as it had at the

landing. I had to pray that the ferryman was right. Though the river looked shallow, I feared deep places. But, having no other way to go, I called on the horse to move toward the other shore.

Testimony of Robert Linnly,
continued

Though I urged the mare forward, she refused to move. Instead she stood, throwing her head, pawing the shallow waters.

"Come on!" I called to her as if she were a person. "Nothing will happen!" I kicked her hard in the ribs.

She would not budge.

Elizabeth, with no notion of what was happening, leaned against me.

I pleaded with the mare, but still she would not move. In desperation I swung myself down and stood in the cold water, finding it no deeper than the calf of my leg. Putting the bridle in Elizabeth's hand, I took hold of the horse's bit.

"We've got to go!" I cried to the mare and began to pull at the bit. At first she refused to move, but when I pulled with all my weight she allowed me to lead her. My arm began to ache, for I would take two steps forward and the horse would take but one. Every inch of the way she held back. And I also had to make sure that Bet did not fall.

The river was not deep—the ferryman had spoken true—the water never came above my knees. But the river bottom was rocky, and I was without shoes. Sometimes the stones were sharp, sometimes slippery. I had to be careful.

I stumbled more than once but always managed to right myself. Each time I tripped, however, I lost the horse's bit. Then the mare would become frightened, back off, and cause me to scramble up to make sure Elizabeth did not lose her place.

Halfway across, I stopped to rest. The passage had become a little easier, or perhaps I had learned how to walk in it, though the cold water did make my legs ache.

Because I was so cold, I hoped the horse would now do as I wanted. Once again, I climbed on the mare's back, letting Elizabeth lean against me. She felt hotter than ever.

"Come on!" I yelled to the horse with a new sense of urgency.

The mare lifted one hoof as if to go, then put it down again.

"You must go!" I shouted, slapping the mare's hind.

This did cause her to move forward skittishly, and for a while I was satisfied with her pace.

"That's it," I encouraged. "Keep going!"

Just when I thought we would get across safely, the mare came to a complete stop.

I became so frustrated that I lost my temper. "Move!" I screamed, giving the horse as hard a blow with my hand as I could.

Frightened, the mare suddenly leaped forward, striking what must have been a slippery rock. Down on her knees she stumbled. Caught by surprise, I started to fall. I clutched Elizabeth, which only caused the two of us to slip off. Fortunately it was no great fall. More startled than hurt, I found myself sitting in the water, Elizabeth by my side. The cold water seemed to waken her momentarily.

But, though we were unhurt, the mare must have cut herself when she stumbled. Clearly she was in pain, and after we fell off, she became confused. She struggled to her legs with a loud whinny, turned about, and frantically made her way back to the side from which we'd come.

"Come back!" I shouted, but to no avail.

Instead, I could see the mare, hobbling, climb the riverbank. There she shook herself, and as if only then sensing her freedom, bolted in between the trees, disappearing from sight.

I sat where we were, angry at the horse's great stupidity. Then my attention returned to Elizabeth. Hauling her up by her arms until she stood erect, I pleaded with her: "You must walk now, Bet. You must."

She was dazed, though perhaps more awake than

before, and I supported her as we moved toward the Easton side of the shore, glancing back in hope of seeing the horse. I could not carry her, and she stood so weakly that we went slowly. "Only a short way," I kept saying. "Just a little more."

After a few slips we did succeed in reaching the other side. I guided her up the bank where it was dry, and let her lie down again. Whatever strength she had found had been spent. Moreover, she had become cold and shivery.

"Bet, listen to me," I said, leaning close to her face. "Can you understand me?"

She seemed to say something, and though I couldn't make it out, I felt she had understood.

"I've got to get the horse," I said. "It won't take long. She can't have gone far. Sleep while I go. I'll be back quickly."

She gave no response.

I looked about to see if anyone was there. But the shore was so wild, so overgrown with trees and shrubs, that I could not see far. So, after making a hurried inspection, I ran back to the riverbank looking for some sign of the mare on the far side.

I saw nothing. Still, I knew what I had to do. Wading into the water, I went as quickly as I could across to where we had started from, all the time looking for signs. Once on the other side, I scrambled up the embankment in the direction the mare had gone.

I moved as I thought the horse might move, back

toward the road, toward the ferry. From time to time I saw hoof marks, but not once did I see the mare. Still, I kept believing she could not be far off.

You must understand that the mare was important to us, the more so with Bet ill and needing to be carried. So I kept going farther, calling to the mare but receiving no kind of answer.

{ 8 }

Testimony of Robert Linnly,
continued

I never did see the horse. Each
time I heard a sound I rushed forward, only to be
disappointed. Then I would remind myself that I
had to go back, that I must not leave Bet alone for
long. But as I did, I also told myself that the horse
was merely a little farther on. Before I realized it, I
was back at the ferry landing—a long way from Bet
and no closer to catching the horse than I had ever
been.

Reluctantly, I decided I could go no farther. The
horse was gone. Having accepted that, I began to
run back through the woods, thinking that perhaps
I'd missed the mare. I was wrong, of course.

Soon I reached the place where we had forded the
river. Without hesitating I waded into the water,
moving as fast as I could. Only when I was mid-river
did I look up toward where Bet lay. To my
astonishment, someone was standing there.

I stopped and stared. Standing over Bet was a

woman—she seemed to be an old woman. Her dirty gray hair hung down loosely, almost touching her waist. Her feet and arms were bare, brown, and looked bruised in places. The clothes she wore were old and soiled. Yet, poorly as she looked, it struck me that her clothing had once been fine, as if it had once belonged to a person of some wealth.

I hurried now, not caring how much noise I made, wanting the woman to see me. I thought I might scare her off. But she remained quite motionless, looking down at Elizabeth.

"Bet!" I hollered. "Bet!"

The woman turned slightly, allowing me to see her face. Although her body had looked old, her face, when first I saw it, seemed young and smooth. For the briefest second, I even thought she was a child.

As I drew nearer, her face changed. What I had first taken to be smoothness became countless tiny lines, drawn tight as a fine net of silk over her skin. Her face was long, and she had a strong nose, thin lips, and high cheekbones.

Like some stupid people I have seen, she kept her mouth half open, as if about to speak, but speak she did not. Her eyes, however, were anything but dumb; they were like no eyes I had ever seen. They were so very blue against that dark and netted face, and like an animal's eyes, they were alert and watchful. But, unlike an animal, she blinked all the time.

I came forward slowly. As I approached, she gently put up a hand of warning.

"Shhhh!" she said, just as if I were entering a room. "She's asleep."

I was greatly puzzled how to act. After a moment I went to Elizabeth and knelt by her side, placing my hand on hers, as if to claim her as mine. I noted that her hand was very hot.

"She's sick," the woman said to me in a rasping whisper. Her breath hung in the air as she peered over my shoulder. "I found her here," she said. "I don't know who she is."

"She is my friend," I explained. "Is your home nearby? Can you help her?"

Blinking, the woman looked at me suspiciously. "Home?" she said, shaking her head as if the question upset her. "Do I have a home? Once I had. A fine home. Someday I'll tell you all about it. Yes, a fine home. Sometimes I speak about it." She spoke very slowly, stressing each word equally. She might have been talking to herself.

"We must do something for my friend," I said, indicating Bet. "She's ill."

"Yes, I see that," the woman agreed. "I was walking when I found her. Why is she all alone? I said to myself. And then I said: The girl is sick. So I said: What kind of sickness does she have? But I didn't know that, so I couldn't answer."

"It's her arm," I told her. "She hurt her arm and it has become bad." I felt I had to talk to her as if she were a child, even younger than myself. I pointed to Elizabeth's arm and pulled back the bandage to show the swollen redness.

The woman leaned down, blinked, and said nothing. She only shook her head.

"*Can* you help her?" I asked.

"Help her?" the woman echoed. "Perhaps I can. Perhaps I can't."

"Please try," I said.

"Yes," said the woman in that odd whisper of hers that forced me to listen carefully. "I was just walking here. I don't usually. No, not here. It's too open here. 'She's sick,' I said. 'A sick child.' I wasn't sure she'd want my help. People don't want me about. People don't want my help." Her voice had dropped so low that I could hardly hear her.

"I want your help," I insisted.

"Do you?" she said, looking up at me in surprise. She seemed to consider for a moment, then abruptly she said, "She will have to come to my home."

"I thought you didn't have a home."

"It isn't a proper home," she murmured, shaking her head. "Not like it once was. All of that is gone. Did you know that? Did someone tell?"

"Please show me where you live," I cried in exasperation. "If it's not far, I'll bring her there."

The woman looked at me as if sometimes she saw me, sometimes not, depending on her thoughts. All the while her eyes blinked and her mouth remained slack. "Very well," she finally said, "I'll show you.

But it's not a proper home," she repeated as if in warning.

So saying, she turned and without a backward glance started to walk into the woods, following no path that I could see. For a moment I was not sure I should follow.

She must have sensed my uncertainty, for she looked around. "Won't you come?" she asked.

There was no other choice. Struggling, I got Bet to her feet, but she could not stand by herself. By placing my arm around her I managed to hold her up, and so we moved one step at a time.

"She'll help you," I whispered into Elizabeth's ear. "She will. I know she will." Why I should have said such a thing I cannot say. I had no idea what the woman would do.

Testimony of Robert Linnly,
continued

The woman did not help me with Elizabeth. Instead she kept some paces ahead. Every few steps she stopped, turned, and looked to see if we were still following. Not once did she speak.

I did my best to hurry, but it was all I could do to hold Bet. Steadily we moved uphill.

At last we came to an area of great trees, trees of a vast height that had never been cut. The ground beneath our feet was covered with a thick mat of damp leaves. This softness underfoot sucked in every sound so that we moved over it silently, as if we had wandered into a great church. The air smelled sweet, and seemed heavy. The tallness of the trees blotted out most of the light, but here and there long rods of sun poked through the branches. They made me think of long, golden fingers, the fingers of God.

I wondered if I was doing the right thing. How I wished I had taken the job when it had been offered to me at the ferry! I should have trusted Mr. Hill, even told him about Elizabeth. More than anything, I wanted to get to Easton, find him, and ask him for work.

As for the woman leading us, the farther she went into the woods, the more anxious I became. I kept wondering where she was going and what she could do to help Bet.

Once I called out: "I've got to rest!" I sat on the ground, placing Elizabeth beside me. The woman never offered to help; she only waited and said nothing.

I confess I thought she might be a witch. Her strange looks and odd clothes made me think it. I had heard of witches, though I had never seen one. The thought startled me, and I grew frightened. But then she looked at me with her open mouth and ever-blinking eyes and I decided it was just a foolish thought.

I came to my feet again, then pulled Elizabeth up. "Not much farther," I whispered, though in truth I didn't know how far we had to go. Still, more than once I said, "Only a little way now."

Just as I was beginning to think the woman would never stop, she halted. We had come up against a kind of bluff, a cliff of rock. Against and along this bluff the woman now began to walk. As the land was level, it was easier for me. Even so, I had again to beg her to pause awhile. Patiently she stopped, but still she said nothing.

After what seemed hours of walking—I don't know how far we came—she stopped and beckoned to me. I set Elizabeth gently against the rocky wall.

"There," the woman whispered, like it was a secret she took delight in telling. "There is my home."

Baffled, I looked where she pointed. I saw nothing that looked like a house.

"I'm sorry," I told her. "I don't see it."

She smiled as if what I said was funny. "I'll show you," she said, and once more continued forward, but faster than before. I had to hurry to keep up. Then I saw it.

At the base of the cliff the stone cut sharply back. Before this undercut a great heap of stones had been placed so that an enclosure had been formed. A gap in this odd wall made it possible to pass through. What one went into was not really a cave, but a bluff cut back so deeply that it felt like a cave, the more so with the ragged wall that ringed it. Looking inside, I could see that it went back a long way. How far, it was difficult to tell.

The front area was no more than twenty feet across, but it ran much deeper. The floor was hard-packed earth. Strangest of all was that the place had been fitted out like the room of a fine house. There were chairs, a table, a bench. I even saw what must have been a cupboard. But everything was broken, tilted, with paint peeling off, like a pretend home that young children might put together from discarded things.

"Do you think it's fine?" she asked, watching me.

"Yes," I replied, not sure what else to say.

"There's a bed back there," she said, pointing to the far end. "The girl may lie there."

No matter what sort of place it was, I gladly led Bet over and let her lie on the bed. It had a straw mattress and even an old blanket, which I pulled over her.

I turned about and studied the place more carefully. In addition to the other furnishings there was a mirror, a picture leaning against a wall, and even a vase. Like everything else, these too were broken. Moreover, in the midst of the supposed room was a mound of ash—an open fire.

As I looked at all these things, the woman watched me, her eyes always blinking. Then she moved very close to me, almost touching. I could feel her breath; smell her.

"Do you know who I am?" she whispered.

Backing away, I shook my head.

"You don't know what they call me?" she asked.

Again I shook my head.

"Moll. Moll is what they call me. Moll isn't my real name. But it goes, you see. Mad Moll. Moll

Mad. Mad Moll. Do you think I'm mad?"

"No, I don't," I managed to say, though she did sort of frighten me.

"Shall I tell you who I really am?" she said into my ear.

"I'm worried about my friend," I protested, trying to back away.

She continued to edge toward me. "Maybe you won't want me to help when you know who I am."

"I don't care," I insisted. "Just help her if you can."

The woman stood there, arms clasped around herself. Then she began to speak in her singing voice, her blinking eyes peering down. "My real— my real name is . . ." She hesitated, then whispered: "Rachel. I mustn't say my other name. *They* don't want me to. No, they don't. I was from Philipsburg. That's across the river. Do you know where it is?"

"No," I told her.

"Ah," she said, but my answer seemed to puzzle her, for she remained silent a long while. Then she started to speak again, though with difficulty. "I was young there," she began, "much younger, and there were wars against the French. That you already knew."

I didn't know what she was talking about. I could only stare at her and say nothing. It didn't seem to matter.

"I was to marry," she continued. "Marry Mr.—

No. I must not say his name either. It would not be liked. It being war and troubled times, soldiers were all about from distant places. One of the soldiers attacked me—then he ran away.

"No one would have me then. No one. I could not stay. How could I? No one wanted me. My parents, the man I was to marry. I came here. I've been here for some time. I don't see people. They don't wish to see me. Sometimes boys come. They call 'Mad Moll! Mad Moll!' That's not my name. I frighten them. Do I frighten you?"

"No," I lied.

"Have you understood what I said?" she asked.

"Help my friend!" I cried out in exasperation. "She's very ill. You said you would help her!"

For a long time she looked at me with her blinking eyes. "I don't know," she said at last. "It was a long time ago. But I shall try."

She went to where the mound of ashes lay and bent low to the ground. Then, with her cheek touching the earth, she began to blow and blow again. In moments there was fire.

{ 10 }

Testimony of Robert Linnly,
continued

I looked on while the woman worked the fire into a full blaze by blowing, coaxing, and adding bits of wood. When it grew large enough to satisfy her, she ordered me to fetch water.

"I don't know where to get it," I said.

She pointed toward the cupboard where a piece of crockery sat, all chipped and black with soot.

I took it down. "Where is the water?" I asked.

"Along the bluff," she said without looking at me.

I went out from under the bluff and through the enclosure. I did not know which way to turn, but since I had not noticed any water as we traveled, I turned in the other direction. Sure enough, along the base of the bluff I found a path.

Not far beyond, I found the place she meant. Out of the face of the rock, from what must have been a hidden spring, water seeped down over the gray stone, making it a shiny black. Down the water spread until it reached an overhang where it collected and dripped as steadily as the ticking of a clock. Yet, once it struck the ground, it completely sank away. Beneath this dripping I placed the pot.

It took a long time to fill the pot. I tried to be patient, but it was difficult. My thoughts were elsewhere. First I tried to make up my mind what to tell the strange woman about us. I wasn't sure she would ask, but I did not wish to be unprepared.

Then my thoughts went back to Mr. Hill, for I was determined to go to Easton. If he still had need of me, I wanted to work for him. We needed money for food. I thought that if Bet could stay with the woman and get better, I could go and work for Mr. Hill.

That made me wonder how long it might be before Bet got well. And only then did I consider that she might not. Such a thought made my head ache. I told myself she would get better because she had to. To have come so far and then to die would be wrong. I wouldn't allow myself to think that she might die.

All these thoughts for which I had no answers made me uncomfortable, so that even though the pot was not full, I snatched it up and ran back to the cave. The woman was waiting. She had made the fire even bigger and its warmth filled the air, taking away some of the dampness.

The woman placed the pot on the ground, close to

the fire, then sat back and watched. I looked about to see if there was any food to be had. Seeing none, I went to where Elizabeth lay asleep and sat down beside her, all the while keeping my eye on the woman.

The light of the flame, its jumping and leaping, seemed to alter her face. Her blinking eyes grew larger, more wondrous than before. And the yellow flame caused her eyes to glow and her hair to seem fair. Her mouth was continually working as if she was chewing, mumbling to herself.

At her feet were piles of things—bits of leaves, bark, and herbs. Perhaps she did know magic. I didn't want to think of that at all, and so I pushed the thought far away.

The woman took pinches of leaf and bark and herbs from the pile and threw them into the pot, using a wooden spoon to mix them. I decided then that I did not care what she was; all that mattered was if she could help Elizabeth.

When the woman had done with her mixing, she lay the spoon aside. Using her dress to shield her fingers she snatched up the pot from the fire and brought it to where Elizabeth lay and I was sitting. I scurried away, but I did not go so far from them that I could not see all she did.

The woman unwrapped Bet's bandage and touched the swollen wound with her fingers. Even that slight touch caused Bet to stir and make a sound. I could see how much the arm pained her.

"What is her name?" the woman asked.

"Elizabeth," I whispered, my mouth dry.

"Elizabeth," the woman echoed, once then twice again. Then she took a corner of her dress and, after dipping it into the hot mix, began to apply it to the swollen places.

"Someone hurt Elizabeth," she began to say, her voice soft, as if she were chanting a song. "Someone hurt her. Who would hurt Elizabeth? Who would dare hurt this girl?" It didn't seem as if she were asking questions, only that these were the thoughts in her head. In any case, I did not answer.

The woman kept wiping the wound with the cloth. Under pressure, it opened. I saw blood begin to flow, blood both red and white. The sight of it made me feel sick.

"I might have had a girl," said the woman, speaking in whispers to Elizabeth, not to me. "A girl like you. Would anyone hurt you? I would not let them. Not I. Not I," she fairly sang.

Though it made me ill, I edged closer to see what was happening. The woman kept dipping the cloth and pressing, bringing forth more blood. It caused Elizabeth to sigh, moan a bit, and try to move.

"Is she all right?" I asked, greatly worried.

"Not I, not I," repeated the woman, as if she had not heard my question, but only one of her own.

"We are runaways," I blurted out without even thinking. "Runaway felons, bonded servants."

Not once did the woman pause in her work or

look at me. I was not even sure she had heard me. Still, I kept talking. I felt I had to say something.

"We were transported from England because we were thieves," I rushed on, wanting her to know the truth. "They sent us to Philadelphia, and a man from Trenton—a Mr. Tolivar—bought us. But we couldn't stay there. We *couldn't*. It was as if we were slaves. When we escaped we had to cross the Delaware River, and she went one way, I another. That was when she hurt her arm. I didn't even know it happened. When I did notice it, we were moving so quickly that I paid it no mind, not thinking it was bad. I truly didn't. You see, we had to get away. Please don't tell about us. Promise you won't."

For a long time the woman said nothing. Nervously I waited. When she did speak it was in whispers, and I had to strain to catch her words.

"Who would hurt Elizabeth?" she said. "Not I. Not I."

I knew then that she had not understood one word of what I'd said.

"Will she get better?" I asked after a while, for the woman had stopped working on Bet's arm. "Can you make her better?"

For the first time since I had begun talking, she turned to look at me. In the shadows there at the back of the place, away from the light, her face seemed much darker than before.

"Can you?" I asked again, looking for her to make some sign.

"I've heard of a bark that makes things well," she answered. "A bark from a tree. I've never found it."

"Bark!" I began to feel desperate. "Shall I fetch a doctor?" I asked.

"Doctor?" she said, shaking her head. "A doctor won't come here. They didn't come before, they won't come now. No one comes here. A few boys come. 'Mad Moll, Mad Moll,' they call. Everyone else keeps away. Nobody comes here. 'Mad Moll!' they cry."

"Don't you understand anything about what I'm saying!" I shouted. "It's Bet I'm talking about. *Not you!* I don't care about you! It's her. Just tell me if you can make her better."

"When I was young," the woman said as if I were not there, "I was very fair. Everybody said so. Everybody came to see me then. But who would see me now? *They* said I was nothing. Nothing at all. Not one would come. Not one!" She leaned close to me, her eyes blinking, her mouth working noisily. "When they see me," she whispered, "they lower their eyes and look away. No. They won't even look at me."

So saying, she turned back to Elizabeth and once again began to bathe the wound.

I was so upset at the way she was acting that I had to get up and walk about. Then I came back to her.

"If I can get to Easton I can have work," I told her. "Would money help?"

"The bark," she said. "Someday I'll find the bark."

"I could buy medicine," I pleaded, finding myself crying out of frustration. "I'm sure I could. There's a Mr. Hill there. He's someone I know. He's a friend. He's certain to help."

But she only bent over Elizabeth and continued with her work. There was nothing for me to do but wait. I sat down, my back against the wall, and tried to calm myself.

After a while she stopped and looked at me. "This girl wants to sleep," she said. She carried the pot to the fire and sat it down. Then she went to the front of her room and stood looking out over the stone wall at the woods and the curious fingers of light that still slipped through. I stood nearby, watching her.

After a long time she came about and returned to Elizabeth's side. She put out a hand and began to stroke Bet's brow.

"You're my daughter," she said to the sleeping Elizabeth. "Will you be her brother?" she asked me.

It was as if we were playing a game. I knew, then, that she was in truth mad.

I shook my head. "No," I said. "I am her friend."

"I'm glad you brought her home," she said. "I had grown worried about her. It was kind of you."

I knew now I could wait no longer. I had to go to

Easton and find Mr. Hill. "I'll go now," I said. "But I'll come back. May I?" I was willing to play her game.

"Come whenever you want," she answered, stroking Elizabeth's hand. "You are my daughter's friend."

"I'll go to Easton," I told her. "Can you tell me how to get there?"

"Just follow the path to the water and beyond. You'll find another path that leads you there."

"I'm going now," I said, backing away. "I'll come back."

"We are always home to friends," she said.

I was absolutely desperate. Spinning about, I dashed out of the cavelike room, and raced toward Easton.

{ II }

Testimony of Robert Linnly,
continued

It was already afternoon, and I had to hurry. Half running, half walking, I went the way the woman had told me, along the base of the bluff, passing the dripping water, until I saw a clearly marked path that led downhill. I took it.

My mind was in a state of confusion with enough worries, and even fearfulness, to make it hurt. A picture of Elizabeth being tended by the mad woman kept filling my mind. *The bark of a tree!* It's true I thought the woman mad, but I didn't think she would do Bet harm. What made me near frantic was that I thought the woman would be able to do nothing for Bet.

I was desperate to find Mr. Hill, the only person in Easton I knew. I was determined to tell him all of what had happened to Elizabeth and me, beg his mercy, and plead for his help.

Down the path I ran, skidding and slipping as I

went. Along my way I saw no houses or people, for which I was grateful.

The path I took down the hill abruptly vanished. None the less, I continued in the same direction until I burst upon a narrow road that ran some way inland from the Lehigh River, which I could now see.

I stopped and looked back up the hill. I understood then that the path I had taken was supposed to be hidden. No doubt the woman had made it herself.

Not wishing to forget the way back, I looked about for some indication that would show me the place. Happily there were some rocks on the ground. Two of these I rolled together, then I pried up a moss-covered rock out of the ground. This rock I rolled over the other two, forming a pile. It was to be my sign that the hidden path was near.

I had not gone far along the road before I came to a small house, a house no bigger in fact than a fair-sized room. Stopping to look at it, I realized that it must be the ferryman's house, for nearby in the river was his boat. Then I saw the old man himself sitting by the far end of the house looking out over the water.

I had no particular reason for avoiding him, but neither did I wish to dally. So I went along easily, as if in no great hurry but also with no desire to pause. Nonetheless he looked up, studied me, and as I was passing called out, "Boy!"

I stopped.

"Thought it was you," he said. "You're the boy with the horse and the sick girl. I suppose you got across the river all right?"

"Yes, sir," I replied, wishing he had not remembered me, but not caring greatly that he had.

"When you have money, then I'll take you," he said with a wave of his hand. "No offense meant."

"No, sir," I said, waiting impatiently for him to be finished talking. When he said nothing more, I hurried on and once out of his sight began to run. Soon after, I entered the town.

It was mid-afternoon when I arrived, and many people were about with much business and movement. It seemed rather a large place, which was pleasing to me. It promised places to stay and work to be had. Still, what I wanted most was to find Mr. Hill.

I went to the center of town in search of an inn such as he had described. I was not to be disappointed. I saw a large building, built of brick, over the door of which hung the king's crown in wood as a sign. I went inside, proceeding at once into the main room. A quick glance informed me that Mr. Hill was not there.

Not wishing to speak to anyone, I moved off into a corner and sat down, willing to wait and see if he came. But, as ever with me, I grew restless. Moreover, I was hungry, and there were smells of good food about. I held myself back for perhaps an hour, then, unable to wait any longer, I approached the tapman at the back of the largest room. He was dispensing food and drink.

"Please, sir," I began.

The man was working on some cups, making them bright, but he looked up all the same. "Yes, boy," he said. "What do you want?"

"I'm looking for a man who said he'd stop here."

"What's his name?"

"Mr. Hill. Nathaniel Hill."

"Ah," he said, remembering. "Mr. Hill. He did arrive today. This morning. You must be the boy he told me to look for."

My hopes soared. "Did he mention me, sir?" I asked.

"He did, he did particular," said the tapman in a friendly fashion. "Said that if you came you were to wait for him and that he'd return. Does that sound like your man?"

I felt a great sense of relief. "Yes, sir, it does. Thank you." I started to go, then returned to ask another question: "Did he say how long he'd be gone?"

"I'm afraid not," said the tapman. "Only that you were to wait."

Happy that I had not, after all, come too late, I went back to my corner content to wait far longer. It was as if just knowing he was expecting me had caused a large problem to go away.

Testimony of Nathaniel Hill,
continued

When I awoke from my sleep it was some time past midday. I rose immediately, returned to the taproom to refresh myself, and while there engaged in conversation with the tapman. Not wishing it to be bruited about that I, a gentleman, was hunting a child, I merely told him that I was from Trenton and that I was in Easton to survey local land with the possibility of settling a planta-tion. After a bit of banter about Jersey as opposed to Pennsylvania, he was free with advice, to which I was forced to listen. When he had finally done I informed him that I was expecting a boy whom I intended to employ, and that if the boy arrived, he was positively to wait for me until my return.

I left the inn with only indefinite plans of procedure. In truth, I had no intent of expending great energy. It was hardly necessary, I thought, and does not suit my temperament. At the time it was merely a question of random looking. After all, I had no absolute assurance that the girl had truly come to Easton. Mr. Tolivar had merely told me that she was believed to be heading there.

I walked about the muddy streets casting my eyes over virtually everyone who passed in hope of discovering something. I learned nothing beyond that Easton was a community which interested me not at all, though it was well situated and filled with merchants. Some people worked the land while others were connected to the mines at Durham, which lay to the south. To me Easton was a crude place, far removed from decent society. No doubt such was the reason why the girl might seek it out, it being so far removed from civilization.

I ambled about to no particular purpose. To tell the truth, I was already in that bored state of mind where one wants something, anything, to happen. In time I found myself on the same road by which I had entered the town, the road that led to the ferry landing. At the edge of town I stopped and looked toward the west, where I could well observe the hills. My understanding was that there were no settlements in the hilly sections, the land being unsuitable for cultivation. Both the ferryman and the tapman had stated this fact. But as I looked at the hills it did occur to me that among them would be good places in which to hide.

On the road ahead of me, I spied the figure of

someone coming toward Easton, toward myself, though the person had not yet seen me. Seeing on the instant that it was a young person, I hastily removed myself from the road and stood behind some trees, from which vantage point I was able to observe the newcomer without myself being seen. In this way I recognized the boy I had met on the other side of the river, the selfsame boy to whom I had offered employment, the lad who had given his name to me as Peter York.

My first impulse was to step forward and greet the boy, for I saw that he was in a great hurry and I had not the least doubt that he was coming to take up my offer of work. Something, however, made me check myself.

What was it?

When I had first seen the boy, he was *with* horse. Now, he was *without*. Why should that have given me pause? Because I also recalled what I had been told—to wit: there were *no* settlements in the western area.

Where, then, had the boy left his horse?

That question made me let the boy pass by without revealing myself. You will have to admit that it was a clever piece of reasoning on my part. It is ever so with me; chance points my way with great clarity.

The boy, as I have said, went by half running, half walking, in a far greater hurry than he had been in the morning, when, he had clearly not been in a rush at all. When he had gone past my hiding place, I came out and watched him head for town.

Perhaps it was my boredom. Perhaps I merely wished a diversion. But my curiosity had been piqued. I decided to follow the boy without letting myself be seen. And so determined was he in his headlong pace that there was hardly a need for me to conceal myself, though naturally I took precautions. I always do.

He led me directly to town. Once there, he stopped. I also halted, interested to see where he would go. All in all there was little hesitation in his movement; he proceeded directly to the inn.

Once more I decided it would be best to wait. If the boy emerged quickly from the inn, it would mean that he had no desire to work for me. If he stayed, it would mean that he would do my errands. Had I not shrewdly told the tapman to make him wait?

I pondered what to do with what I had observed. None of it in itself was of any particular value. After all, a fair number of hours had passed since I had last seen the boy. Indeed, he could have gone to the home of his relation, left the horse, and merely brought himself to Easton. The question was: *Where did the relation live?*

As I contemplated this question it occurred to me that there was in fact someone I could ask—the ferryman. He was, I recalled, disposed to chatter. And the boy had told me he was planning to cross by ferry.

Thus I reversed myself once again, on horse this time, covering the distance with ease until I reached the ferry landing. There I found the old man asleep against a small hovel, which I presumed to be his place of dwelling.

"You, sir!" I hailed him.

Starting from his sleep, the old man looked up at me. "Afternoon," he said. "Will you be wanting to cross?" was his automatic question as he hauled himself clumsily to his feet. "Two pennies to go." Only then did he recognize me.

"Oh, it's you!" he said. "That wasn't much of a visit. Thought you said you'd be staying awhile."

"You presume too much," I let him know sharply. "I merely wish some information from you."

"Ask all you want," said the man, clearly disappointed. "Won't do no harm to ask." He settled himself on the ground again.

I was annoyed by his attitude and had a mind to show him how to speak to a gentleman, but since I wanted answers, I let his behavior go by.

"Do you recall," I asked, "that as I crossed the river on your boat this morning I inquired about a girl?"

"What of it?"

"Perhaps it was, after all, a boy I was looking for," I said. "Did a boy cross over with you today?

It would not have been long after you brought me across."

The ferryman considered. "A boy cross over? No, I don't think so." His answer was not a yes or a no.

"Quite sure?" I demanded, growing irritated.

"There was a boy *wanting* to cross with me," he said. "But that's not crossing *with* me, is it now?"

"Why didn't he?"

"No money. But I saw him a short time ago this side, I did. That's right. See, I had to tell him that if he couldn't pay my toll, he had best go up the river where there's a fording place. I daresay that's what they did."

"*They?*" I dared to ask. "You said he was alone."

"I said no such thing. When I saw him now, he was alone."

I swung down from my horse and strode up to where the old man lay. "Be so kind," I said with great politeness as I helped him to his feet, "as to provide me with simple answers. Explain yourself."

No doubt the firmness of my voice and grasp encouraged the man.

"Well, sir," he said, "he was alone when I just saw him, but no, he wasn't alone when I *first* saw him. Over on the other side he even had a horse. And there was a girl with him too, a sick girl."

"A girl!" I cried, holding him firmly.

"Isn't that what I said!" insisted the man. "Looked sick too, she did. Claimed she was sick, the boy did, but I couldn't take them. Why, if I took everyone who begs a ride, why there's no telling what would become of me. I'm a poor man."

"What did the girl look like?" I demanded.

The ferryman proceeded to describe the girl in such a way that I was all but sure it was none other than Elizabeth Mawes.

"Did you ask the boy when he passed by just now," I wanted to know as I let him go, "where the horse and the girl were?"

The ferryman brushed himself off. "That wasn't my business, now was it?"

"Perhaps not," I admitted, not wishing to prolong the interview. "I thank you for your assistance," I said and tossed him a coin, which he took up greedily enough. "I beg you keep our discussion confidential," I warned him, "lest I have to take back that coin with interest." Turning, I began to hurry back toward Easton.

I admit that in the midst of my elation, I was somewhat puzzled. Mr. Tolivar had distinctly told me that the girl had escaped with a boy but that the boy had been retaken. I began to see that I had erred in being unconcerned about the runaway boy, having learned nothing of his particulars—not even his name.

I further understood that the boy who called himself Peter York might be no more than someone Elizabeth Mawes met along her way. Regardless, the girl was a runaway, and the boy was fair game for whatever I chose, as he was helping her escape.

I decided to treat the boy with great caution so as not to frighten him off. If he knew where the girl was hiding, I would get him to lead me to her. If she was indeed ill, so much the better—she would stay put until I came to fetch her.

Having reached these conclusions, I thought it was time for me to make myself known to the local authority. Accordingly, when I reached Easton once more, I hailed the first man I met and requested that he tell me where I might find the local constable.

"You'll be wanting Mr. Clagget," I was told. "Down by Spender's Way. He's your man."

I hastened in the direction the man had indicated.

{ 13 }

Testimony of Mr. George Clagget,
Constable of Easton

I am George Clagget, Esquire, of Northampton County.

I wish to state even before I begin the particulars pertaining to the circumstances which follow that I acted only in accordance with the laws and statutes as set forth in the Commonwealth of Pennsylvania.

A man in my position is not in the way of understanding motives, only acts. That regrettable events did occur I should be the last to deny, but such events, after all, had nothing whatsoever to do with me other than I am an innocent, humble upholder of the law. I am certain Your Excellency shall see that for yourself, but I wish to take pains to point it out.

During the afternoon of April 13, 1768, instant, I was within my office tending to my heavy duties, as well as to my business. You should know that I am a lawyer as well as a constable. Indeed I am the only lawyer in Easton and would be pleased to furnish testimonials regarding my character and general fitness if these are so desired.

While I was thus pursuing my tasks I was informed by my good wife that a Mr. Nathaniel Hill wished to speak to me on a subject of particular weight. The name meant nothing to me. Nonetheless, I asked that he be shown in, for it is the policy of my office that I extend a courtesy to all who apply. This may be a fault.

Shortly thereafter, Mr. Hill entered my rooms. We exchanged normal civilities and then Mr. Hill opened with his business.

"I've only just arrived in Easton," he informed me. "I am a resident of Trenton, in Jersey Colony."

I remarked that he was a long way from home and hoped that I could be of some service to him. Asking him to be seated, I begged him to be frank with me.

"I am under the employ of Sir John Tolivar of Trenton," he began. "No doubt you know of him."

I had to confess that I never had the honor of knowing this man Tolivar.

Mr. Hill went on to inform me that Sir Tolivar was a highly placed individual in the affairs of Jersey government, that he owned considerable land, and that he had under contract a great number of servants. One of these, it seems, was a girl named Elizabeth Mawes, who was a branded felon. According to Mr. Hill, she was transported by His Majesty's court to the colonies under contract of labor for a period until she came of age at twenty-one. In short, the man Tolivar owned her. Notwithstanding all this, she had, so Mr. Hill explained, run away and was believed to have come to Easton. Mr. Hill said that as a personal favor to Sir Toliver—and at no small expense of his own—he had come to find her and bring her back.

Hearing all this, I informed Mr. Hill that I had received no information concerning the girl.

"*I* am able to inform you about her," said Mr. Hill. "What is more, I have already determined that she did come to Easton and is hiding hereabouts."

I asked him if he was sure of his facts.

"Not proof positive," he allowed, "but I expect to have that soon enough. I merely thought I had best inform you of this matter so that when I do learn exactly where she has hidden herself, you will, as required by your position, help me apprehend her."

I asked him if he had papers to prove that this Sir Tolivar had a right to the girl.

"I do not have them on my person," he said. "They are safe in my saddlebags at my lodging. I am staying at the inn. Fetching them for you is a matter of moments."

I informed Mr. Hill that he was, of course, free to go and come as he liked but that, with all due respect, I did require some proof that the girl *was* a runaway felon before I could aid him in her capture. This he understood.

"I shouldn't think of troubling you," he allowed,

"other than for something perfectly legal. I shall be more than happy to show you the proper papers. I came today mainly to inform you of my actions so that when I do find the girl—and I shall find her shortly—you will understand my situation. Of course Sir John Tolivar shall hear of your kindness in providing assistance." Without further ado he stood and held out his hand. "I thank you," he said, "for your time and interest."

We shook hands, and I accompanied him to the door. As he was leaving he seemed to recall something else.

"There is one question I had," he said. "West of the Ferry, along the Lehigh River, are there many dwellings?"

I informed him that to the best of my knowledge no one had settled in that quarter, that the soil was considered so ill suited, with such a vast array of stone within the earth, that the area had never been looked on with favor. Indeed, I particularly recall telling him that the land was so bad that, as far as I knew, the only one who resided there was an unhappy woman who knew no better in her mind and was best let alone.

He expressed an interest in this person and asked to know more about her.

I told him I was hardly the person to ask. All I could tell him was that she was known as "Mad Moll" and was considered harmless. Indeed, I confessed that I myself had never seen her nor felt any reason, private or professional, to seek her out.

At these words he shook hands with me once again and took his leave.

That was the entire extent of our first interview. As you can see with clarity, I acted properly, my behavior being exactly as it should have been.

{ 14 }

Testimony of Robert Linnly,
continued

I waited for a long time at the inn.
More than once I was tempted to leave, worried as I
was about Bet. Twice I left the building and stood
out front, in hopes that Mr. Hill would arrive,
vowing to leave if he did not. But each time I went
back inside. The truth is, I could not think how else
to get help other than by waiting for Mr. Hill.

As the afternoon wore on and he did not return I
grew ever more hungry. It had now been more than
twenty-four hours since I had last eaten. When I
could not restrain myself any longer I approached
the tapman and offered to do some work for him.

"Hasn't your man arrived yet?" he asked.

"No, sir."

"Don't worry about it," he said. "He will. He told
me for certain that you were to wait and that he'd
come. No mistake about it. Just be patient."

I spoke out. "Would it be possible, sir," I asked,

"for me to do some work for you in exchange for something to eat? It's been a day since I've eaten."

He looked at me. "A master who leaves you without food. That's not very nice, and him a gentleman. Well, you might do something." He looked about in search of a needful task. "You can sweep the floor clean if you've a mind to. I'll give you something for that—not much, mind—but enough to keep you."

Gladly I took the offered broom and began to work in earnest. The tapman must have been pleased with me because even before I'd done he gave me a large piece of bread to chew on as I worked. This I did, though I saved a part of it to give to Bet.

It took the good part of an hour to clean the place, but when I was done the man was satisfied. Taking back his broom he laid out a large plate of food and drink for me at a side table and stood there while I ate. He seemed to take pleasure in watching me eat.

"This boy won't be an easy one to keep," he said, laughing at how much and how quickly I ate. He was addressing a man who was sitting nearby. "He works hard, but he eats just the same." It was not said in an unkindly fashion.

"Yes, sir," I replied, though I could not have held back my eating even if I had wanted to.

"Your master," continued the tapman, "will find a difference between Pennsylvania and Jersey lads, I'll swear. I take you for a Pennsy boy. Well, he'll wish he brought over a Jersey boy with him, one who doesn't eat so much." And again he laughed.

His words made me stop eating. I stared up at him. "*Jersey?*" I asked, almost choking on my food.

"Yes, Jersey," said the tapman. "Hasn't he just come from there, from Trenton? That's what he told me, anyway. All I was saying," he said, misunderstanding why I was upset, "and no offense, boy, for you're a hard worker, is that I'm willing to wager that a Jersey boy wouldn't fill himself as much as you've done." Then he laughed again before going back to his post.

The words *Jersey* and *from Trenton* broke over me like hard blows. The possibility of what it might mean made my heart beat fast. Instantly I recalled Mr. Hill's questions to me at the ferry. Had he not asked me my name, and whether or not I was alone?

I sprang from my chair, unable to eat any more. In truth a great fear had come upon me, and I made up my mind to flee from the place. Shoving what food I could into my pockets, I headed for the door. I had taken only three steps, when Mr. Hill entered the room.

The two of us stood there looking at one another. Though I was thoroughly frightened, I tried to keep it from showing. It was he who spoke first.

"You've turned up after all," he said. "That's good. Have I kept you waiting long?"

"No, sir, not long," I was able to reply, despite my being incapable of moving.

"Been most diligent in waiting, he has," cried the tapman from his place across the room. "Waiting a few hours. I trust you won't mind, but he did some work for me to satisfy his hunger. And a good bit of hunger it was too, which is understandable considering he hadn't eaten for twenty-four hours. Why, even his pockets are full!"

"Well done!" Mr. Hill said to me. "That speaks well of you. I take it your relation has no objection to your working for me these few days?"

Unable to speak, I could only stare at him. All that afternoon I had built my hopes on him as the one person in all the world who could help us. Now I had to stand there and think just the opposite, that he was the one person we had most to fear from.

The very thought caused a wall of fear to rise up around me, a sense of being trapped. Yet, even then I sensed that if it were true—if he was indeed looking for us—I *had* to stay with him. It was my duty to lead him *away* from Bet. For the one thing I was certain about was that he had no notion as to who I was. How could he? Was he not treating me with ease, offering me work? No, I was convinced he did not know about me.

"Here, boy, I've asked you a question," said Mr. Hill, breaking into my thoughts. "Will you or won't you work for me these few days?"

"Yes, sir," I answered. "I will."

"Good! I'll use you well," he cried, and advancing, he clapped me on the shoulder and turned me toward the table. "Now we two shall sit, and I'll tell you of my business."

He urged me to a seat, then sat down himself. "Did you have enough to eat?" he wanted to know.

"Yes, sir," I returned, not for a second taking my eyes from his face.

"I'm hungry myself," he told me. "So if you've no objection, we'll talk over food."

"No, sir," I replied.

Mr. Hill called the tapman and arranged a meal for himself. Then he settled back in his chair and looked at me, a slight smile on his face. After a moment he said; "Is your relation in good health?"

"Yes, sir," I answered, trying to fix my thoughts. "He said I might work for you until you leave."

"Very much obliged, I'm sure. My compliments to him," said Mr. Hill. "As far as I'm concerned, you may go back to him at the end of each day's work. I shan't need you at night. You can always rejoin me in the morning."

"Go home each day?" I asked, no longer able to look him in the face.

"Why not?" he said grandly. "It's not far, is it, this place where your relation lives?"

"No, sir," I whispered. "Not far at all."

"In town?"

"Just outside."

"Well then, no problem there." He smiled again.

"I'm a liberal master and like to make the best of terms. Now then, I must tell you what has brought me here and what your duties shall be."

So saying, he began to tell me all about a search for land in and around the town, which he was undertaking. Outwardly I listened, but inwardly I was desperately trying to imagine who he might be.

Testimony of Robert Linnly,
continued

While Mr. Hill ate his meal, he informed me of my duties. My suspicions became even more raised when he said nothing to me about coming from Jersey. Instead, all he asked me to do were a few small things like tending to his horse and keeping his boots and room in decent order. It was as if he wished only to keep me about, rather than put me to a proper use.

"Do you think you can do what I ask?" he wanted to know.

"Yes, sir. Can I do anything for you now?" I asked, eager to break away from him.

"You're a good lad for asking," was his reply. "You may go to my room and lay a fire. It may be a goodly town, this Easton, but it's low and damp. Tend to that fire. And when you're done," he added as an afterthought, "bring down my saddlebags. I'll need them."

"Yes, sir. At once."

Hurriedly I asked the tapman where Mr. Hill's room was located and where I would find the storing place for wood. On his directions I fetched wood, took up a candle, and went to Mr. Hill's room.

It was a small room, very white, a white made yellowish by the burning candle in my hand. There were hardly any furnishings: a bed, a chest at the foot of the bed, a chair. The fire was at the far side. As for Mr. Hill's possessions, I saw nothing save the saddlebags he had asked me to bring down.

Going directly to the hearth, I laid out the wood as best I could. Then I set the candle flame to it and remained till the fire took hold and filled the room with warmth.

I looked at the saddlebags, wondering if they contained anything that would help me know for certain who Mr. Hill was. After a quick check to see that Mr. Hill was still at table, I went to the bags, undid the clasps that held them shut, and plunged my hand within.

Cold metal touched my fingers, and I withdrew a double-barreled pistol. A second reach allowed me to find the powder bag and shot. Finding nothing else that side, I put them back and tried the other bag. There my hand touched paper. I withdrew it carefully.

That it was a document I could see at once, for it was covered with writing and had both seals and signatures at the bottom. I do not read that well, and the handwriting was not clear, so it was not possible for me to fully understand what it meant. One part was perfectly clear, however, even to me. Spelled out and writ large was the name

ELIZABETH MAWES

It made my breath stop up to see Bet's name there. Although I did not know exactly what the paper was, it was all the proof I needed that Mr. Hill *was* seeking Elizabeth. Why my name was not also listed on the document I did not know, but I took it as further proof that Mr. Hill had no notion as to my identity.

With the finding of the paper my worst fears about Mr. Hill turned true. How could I have further doubts? Hastily, I plunged it back into the bag.

I composed myself as best I could and returned below with the bags in hand to where Mr. Hill was sitting. "I've done, sir," I told him, handing him his bags. "The fire's lit."

"Thank you," he said politely. Then, to my astonishment, he put aside the pipe he had been smoking, undid one side of the saddlebags, and withdrew the pistol.

For a horrible moment I thought he was about to arrest me. Instead, he turned around and laid the gun on the table. Then he began to work over it with great care, first cleaning and then loading it.

It was a beautifully worked pistol, and one in

which he obviously took great pride. Double-barreled, with two triggers, it was so very bright that it looked new, though he informed me that it was not. As I watched him load it, he took particular pains to tell me that he never knew when he might have need to use it.

"I'm not a man for early rising," he said as he worked, "so you must not come too early tomorrow. If you get here before noon, tend to my horse. We shall have all the time we need to undertake what I intend to do." He patted the pistol. "Perhaps I can even do some hunting. I should like to show you how well I can use this gun."

I merely nodded to show I understood.

"I hope," he said, "that all of this is perfectly clear to you. Have you any questions?"

"No, sir."

"Then you had best be off," he said, even as he finished with his gun. "Just see to my horse—make sure she's fed and brushed." He tapped his pistol to his brow by way of salute. "Remember, my compliments to your relation. I'll look for you by noon."

"Yes, sir," I whispered. "Good night, sir."

I left somewhat clumsily. In truth, he had greatly frightened me, and my legs were like straw.

Once outside, I was of two minds. I wanted to go directly to Bet, though by now there was hardly enough light for me to see. I feared that, despite the markers I had left, I might lose my way.

I stood there trying to make up my mind. Then

for some reason I glanced behind me. Mr. Hill was observing me through the window. Alarmed, I moved instantly toward the stable as he had bade me do.

After Mr. Hill's horse was pointed out to me, I fed her, made sure she had water, brushed her down, and left. It was now almost completely dark.

I had to make certain that Mr. Hill was not following me, and so I moved down the main street in a direction opposite to where I wanted to go. I went slowly, openly. Now and then I stopped at various buildings and gawked at them, glancing backward toward the inn. But of Mr. Hill I saw no sign.

When I reached the far northern edge of town I stood beside a building and, waiting, poked my head out a few times to see if he would come. He did not.

Sure that I had not been followed, I went back through the town again, not by main streets but by alleyways. I reached the other end of town certain that I had not been watched.

Down the road to the ferry I went. The early moon provided just enough light for me to see, but I knew I would not be able to find my way back to Bet that night. Still, I was determined to get as close as possible, find a place to sleep, and in the early morning proceed to the cave room by the markers I had made.

I went easily, free now of any thoughts of being

followed. My mind was full of questions as to what we might do. If only Bet were well, we could instantly move on. But I knew that was impossible.

On I walked until I made out the ferryman's house. I knew it was just before the hidden path, so I lay down by the edge of the road. I must have been very tired, for I fell asleep at once.

{ 16 }

Testimony of Nathaniel Hill,
continued

That first evening in Easton, áfter the boy left, I watched him from the window of the inn, having already determined that I would make no attempt whatsoever to follow him. My reasoning was this: I wished him to be completely at his ease, without any doubts or fears regarding me or his relationship to me. Only in such a way could I have him lead me to the girl.

It must be understood that at this time I still had no evidence as to who *he* was. Remember yet again that I had been informed that the runaway boy had been caught!

But here was a boy who had told me himself that he was traveling alone, only to be seen shortly afterward with a girl who fit the general description of the one I sought. The boy's very manner and circumstance—as I recalled the first time we met—grew ever more damning in my mind. And had he not told the tapman that he had not eaten in twenty-four hours? What kind of "uncle" would treat him so, would require him to bulge out his pockets with the tapman's bread? In short, all that I knew appeared to justify my suspicious thoughts.

On top of that I believed him to have no notion as to who I was. My desire, as you can see, was to trick him into leading me to the girl. Was not that the best thing to do? *Of course it was!*

When I saw him stride off to the stable, I returned to my table and took my drink and pipe in leisure. I had every reason to be pleased. I do not pretend that I had not been fortunate. It is an ill-mannered man who does not acknowledge Fortune when she winks at him. Still, it would have given me great pleasure to resolve the matter simply, with little fuss or effort. In truth, I was eager to go home.

The tapman came over. "Is everything satisfactory?" he inquired.

I told him it was.

"That's a willing, pleasant lad you have," he offered.

"I think so," I returned. "He says he's from hereabouts. Says he's got a relation here."

"Does he?" said the tapman, surprised. "He didn't tell me that, and I've never seen him about before. What's his name?"

"He gave it as Peter York."

The tapman shook his head. "Don't know any folks by that name, and I like to think I know most everybody hereabouts. Perhaps his relation is on his mother's side and has her name."

In my mind I decided to consider this point, which to now had escaped me.

"Can you tell me," I resumed, "about a woman known as Moll? Mad Moll, I think she's called."

"Oh, you've heard about her," said the tapman with a grin. "Yes, there's a story. She's a strange one, and nobody doubts she's mad. She doesn't come down here, mind, so I can't swear it to you. But they say—it's only the boys who like to tease her who get to see her, and even they don't know where she lives—that she's completely daft."

"Who is she?"

"They say she was from a good family across the river in Jersey. Philipsburg, I believe. She was all set to marry someone when she was raped by a soldier. Her intended would have naught to do with her after that. She fled over to this side of the river and tucked herself away in the hills swearing, or so they say, never to show herself again. I've heard tell she was a beauty once. But there aren't many who can truly say they've ever seen her."

"Is she really mad?" I wanted to know.

He shrugged. "You hear stories."

"And no one knows where she keeps herself?" I wondered.

Again the tapman shook his head. "I doubt it. Between you and me, people think it's best to let her be, poor soul. I don't see how she's liable to be anything but harmless. May the Lord protect her, say I. Why do you ask?"

"I heard someone speak of her," I explained evasively. "Since I intend going through the hills, I thought I might come upon her."

"Not her," insisted the tapman. "She may see you, but you won't know it. She keeps her distance."

When the tapman left, I considered what he had said. If the girl was ill, and so the ferryman had reported, I asked myself where the boy might have taken her. Perhaps to the mad woman, a woman moreover who was said to have naught to do with anyone save children.

The whole thing seemed fairly easy. I considered that Mr. Tolivar's reward money was already in my pocket, and so I took my pleasure at cards that night. I did splendidly, which I took as the best of omens.

{ 17 }

Testimony of Robert Linnly,
continued

I did not sleep well. Though it had been a warm night, I had been restless and woke at first light feeling damp and chilly. For a while I lay on my back, staring vacantly about. A thin, shredded mist clung to the roots of trees, and the treetops glowed with the early light of dawn. These first rays of light seemed to be trying to reach down through the high timber. Once again I was reminded of great fingers, prowling, poking, silent fingers in search of things to grasp.

As I lay there the light increased and birds began to chatter. That in turn woke every other living thing. Where but a moment before I thought I was alone, I soon became only one among many.

I got up and stepped out onto the road. The place where the ferryman lived was close by, but I saw no sign of him.

Once more I began to walk westward, going

quietly past the hut till I reached the path along the river and found the rocks I had piled up. As I had hoped, they were easy to recognize. There I turned into and behind the bush, found the proper path, and followed it up toward Bet.

There was no difficulty. The path was faintly marked, but I was able to follow it. Before me I could see the higher hills and knew that I had gone correctly, that the bluff would not be far ahead. When I reached the cliff I began to hurry along its base, passing by the dripping water. Soon I saw the wall-like structure the woman had heaped before the rock.

Everything was still. The smell of burning wood filled the air. I could even see the shimmering heat against the rockface moving up on the morning currents. Cautiously I went on till I reached the entranceway. Looking in, I found myself staring into the eyes of the woman.

It was as if she had been waiting for me. She was sitting close to the fire but was looking directly at the entrance where I stood. Her face now seemed old and worn, without any warmth. She blinked from time to time, and her slightly open mouth worked silently.

I said nothing to her, nor did she speak to me. We merely looked at one another.

"Is she any better?" I finally asked, trying to look past her into the back area. Only dimly could I see the bed and the shape of Elizabeth lying there.

The woman seemed not to have heard. I repeated my question. "Is she all right?"

When she did answer me her voice sounded raspy, as if she had not talked for a long time. "My daughter is sleeping," she announced.

I sighed at the woman's delusions. "May I go to her?" I asked. "I brought her some food." I took the bread, now mostly stale, from my pocket.

"She's not well," replied the woman.

"Worse?" I asked at once.

The woman gave no answer, so I didn't wait for permission. Instead, I hurried back until I stood beside the bed.

Elizabeth was lying on her back covered with the old blanket, arms exposed at her side, the right hand open, revealing the branded thumb. The wound was unbandaged, and while it didn't look as bad as it had yesterday, it was still swollen and red.

Her face was pale, almost white in the framed darkness of her hair and the dullness of the place. Her lips seemed almost chalk. Her eyelids fluttered now and then.

For a frightful moment I thought that she was dead. I put my ear close to her mouth. Only then did I catch the faint shallowness of her breath.

I put my hand to her cheek. My hand was cool, but her face seemed colder yet. I took the bread from my pocket and held it so that she could smell it, and even touched it to her lips. She did not react at all.

"Please get well," I whispered.

Seeing that she would not eat, I ate the bread myself. After sitting by her for a while I felt compelled to talk. "Can you hear me, Bet? It's me, Robert." I looked around to see if the woman was close, but she wasn't. She had remained by the entrance.

"There's a man, Bet. He's looking for you. But he doesn't know who I am. I think we should get away. Do you think so?"

She lay as silently as before.

"I know you're too sick to move," I said. "I'll go back to Easton and make sure he can't find you. You'll be perfectly safe here." As I spoke I kept watching for her to make some sign, any sign, that she heard me, but she gave none. "Bet," I said, "I promise he won't find you. I promise."

I got up and went back to the woman. She hadn't moved. I sat down directly in front of her so that she could not avoid me.

"Is she going to get better?" I wanted to know.

The woman said nothing.

"*Please*, you must tell me," I insisted. "I have to know."

"When I was young," the woman began in a whisper, just as if she hadn't heard a word I had said, "when I was young I was fair. I lived in a house. My mother and father looked after me. Such a long time ago. Can you remember that?"

"I didn't know you then," I answered wearily.

"*Everybody* knew me then," she insisted. "How could you not?"

"I just came yesterday. With Elizabeth. Don't you remember that? Just yesterday."

The woman lifted her eyes to look at me, then cast her glance down again. "I try to forget everything," she said in a whisper. "But I can't." She shook her head. "I remember everything. *Everything.*"

"Can you remember what I told you about us?" I shouted. "We're runaways. Do you remember that!" I had grown angry.

"No," she said simply, softly. "I don't like to remember things. Yet I always do. I remember the books I read. Shall I tell you about them?"

"There's a man come," I tried to tell her, wanting to scream I was so angry. "He's come for Bet. I know he has!"

That time the woman lifted her eyes. Something I had said had reached her. "Come for her?" she repeated, her eyes blinkly rapidly.

"Elizabeth!" I shouted.

"My *daughter?*" she said as faint as breath.

Not knowing what else to say, I nodded.

"To *take her?*" she asked.

"Yes," I insisted.

"I won't let him," she returned, her voice suddenly rising to a shrillness. "I shan't. I mustn't. I won't let them! I . . ." Abruptly her voice trailed off helplessly, and her eyes looked down again.

"I think we should move her," I said. "Go somewhere else. I'll help you. We could do it now."

"No," the woman said after a time. "My daughter is not well. She's ill. What I need to do is find the proper bark from that tree." Turning, she looked back to where Bet lay. "Yes," she said, "the proper bark." Then she looked at me and her eyes widened in surprise. She leaned forward, her face close to mine, her breath coming quickly. "*Who are you?*" she whispered.

My hopes collapsed. "I'm her friend," I answered stupidly. "Her friend."

"Yes," she nodded, withdrawing her face from mine. "Children are my friends." Then she closed her eyes and began to hum.

I looked out at the sky. It was growing late. I knew I had to go back to Easton.

"I'll come again tomorrow," I said, standing up. "Perhaps tonight."

Her eyes were still closed and she seemed to be singing a song. It was as if she were already alone.

I stayed only long enough to look again at Elizabeth. I had to force myself to go, but when I did, I raced along the base of the bluff.

{ 18 }

Testimony of Robert Linnly,
continued

I hurried back to Easton. Sometimes I walked, sometimes I ran, for I wanted to get to Mr. Hill before he awoke. I knew I could not move Bet. That meant I had no choice but to try to keep Mr. Hill away from her.

When I reached Easton I went straight to the inn. I looked into the main room, and when I saw that Mr. Hill was not there I hurried to the stable and attended to his horse. I found him waiting for me when I came out. My first thought was that he had watched me come.

"Good morning," he greeted me.

I wished him a good morning as well.

"You've arrived early, I see," he said. "I appreciate that. I got up sooner than I had expected myself. Have you had your breakfast?"

"No, sir."

"Then come and join me. I expect we shall have a long day."

We went into the taproom. With a motion of his hand he indicated that I was to sit and eat. Needing no second invitation, I ate a good breakfast.

When Mr. Hill had completed his meal, he sat back and looked at me closely. "Now then," he began, "we've our work to do. I shall need to see the land to the south, to the west, and to the north of Easton. The only place I'll not look is across the river in Jersey. My land search will take a few days, and so we shall have to choose each area as we go. Now, young sir, do you have any notion which way to start?"

"No, sir, I don't," I mumbled.

"Your relation," he said. "Where has he settled? And by the by, is he related on your father's or your mother's side of the family?"

"Father's," I said quickly, wishing I had never made up the tale.

He nodded in understanding. "And he farms?"

"Yes, sir," I said, puzzled that he should ask such things.

"Where?" he demanded.

I was not sure how to answer, but thinking that perhaps he had seen me come in from the west, I felt obliged to answer that way. "To the west of town," I replied.

"Does he do well?" he continued. "Things grow with ease?"

"Not very," I found myself saying, looking for some way to discourage these thoughts. "He finds it too hilly."

"There's a point," agreed Mr. Hill. "The land does rise. I saw so myself. I'll have to consider that." He sat back in his chair and looked at me. "Perhaps," he said after a moment, "I might even speak with this uncle of yours and gain his advice. Do you think that might be possible?"

"I don't know," I managed to say, unsettled at the drift of his talk.

"Well, would you be kind enough to ask him for me?"

"Yes, sir," I felt compelled to answer.

"Good! Now then, I should like you to attend to my room and then return here. Bring my pistol, shot, and powder. We'd best take the pistol with us—no telling who or what we might meet."

I got up slowly, trying hard to think what to do. I felt myself being squeezed, placed in a situation from which I could find no escape. What I wanted to do was simply bolt—get Bet away from where she was, whatever it took. Even so, I reminded myself that Mr. Hill did not know who I was, that I had to stay in town and keep him away from her.

I slowly climbed to the second floor and went to his room. I did his bed first, putting it to some degree of neatness. Then I placed the chair against the wall. Finally, I took the saddlebags he had placed beneath the bed and drew them out.

After a moment's hesitation, I opened the bag and sought the document I had found earlier, having the sudden impulse to put it to the fire. The document was gone. Hastily I checked the other side. The pistol was there, but no document.

I decided to take this as a good sign, concocting the notion that Mr. Hill was merely *delivering* the paper that bore Bet's name, that he did not have any intention of using it himself. I so wanted to think that everything was well!

I went down again with the saddlebags. He pulled out the pistol and examined it, all the while chatting about how he liked to shoot, and what a fine marksman he was.

"I have made my decision," he announced. "We shall go north today. Bring the horse around and place the saddlebags on her." He handed them to me.

I was greatly relieved by his decision to go north, for it gave me the feeling that I had more time. My sense of being trapped was eased. I did as I had been told and brought the horse. He mounted, drew me up behind, and in moments we were off.

He seemed in no particular hurry. Taking the first open trail, he urged his horse on easily. He spoke but little, and when he did, it was only about the land. From time to time he asked a question about the area. I tried to give reasonable answers, but I had to invent them. Still, not once did he say anything to make me feel he saw through my lies.

By mid-afternoon he said we had gone far enough and turned the horse's head. He was weary, he claimed, and had no desire to see more.

Only one thing that happened made me nervous again, and it happened as we came back. As we were going along, Mr. Hill drew out his pistol and informed me that he would look for a decent dinner.

Sure enough, as we rode along, two pheasants flew up from almost beneath his horse. With great swiftness he worked his pistol. Two quick reports followed one upon the other. The birds tumbled in midair, feathers exploding in all directions.

"Fetch them," he told me.

I leaped down and ran to where I saw the birds fall, took them up, and brought them back.

"Now you load the pistol," he said, handing it to me.

I looked up at him, surprised.

"Who knows what we'll meet," he insisted. "Go on."

Under his watchful eyes and instruction, I did as he told me. I suppose I did the job tolerably well, for we went forward again.

The incident meant two things to me—Mr. Hill was pleased with himself, and he was fine with his pistol. I could not help but wonder if he had shot the birds for his dinner, as he claimed, or to impress upon me his skill with the pistol. I rather thought the latter, and indeed it left me with no doubt as to what he could do, given the opportunity. In moments like these I felt he was toying with me, which gave me a feeling akin to nausea.

There was no other untoward incident. All in all the journey was so relaxed that I confess I began to think I was wrong about him. Perhaps, I chided myself, he was no more than he claimed to be; perhaps he was *no* threat to Bet or myself, and might even help us. It was what I wanted to believe, but I dared not act on my thoughts one way or the other.

You can see how my mind ran from one place to another. I recall once seeing a cat corner a mole. The mole, blind, knew not which way to turn, and took one step one way and one another, until, frightened beyond all control, it merely curled itself into a ball and waited for it knew not what. So like that mole was I.

"I've not seen much of any interest to me," announced Mr. Hill as we came back into town. "Would you say your uncle's land is worse than what we observed today?"

"I think so," I hastened to say.

"Then it's poor indeed. Well, there's tomorrow," he said, "Perhaps you'd be good enough when you return home tonight to present my compliments to your worthy uncle and beg permission for me to visit him. Not for tomorrow, mind. I rather think we should go south tomorrow unless it rains. It looks as if it might rain. But the day after, certainly. Do you think it will be possible for me to see your uncle then?"

"I don't know," I said, unable to find a better answer. "I'll ask."

"Only if it's no trouble, mind," he added. "I should not wish to put your kind relation to any bother."

Saying no more on the subject, he led us to the inn. He directed me to see to the horse, after which, he told me, I was free to go.

It was only late afternoon, and the light was still bright enough to make me think I could reach Bet before dark. I was glad of that, for it did look like rain and I had no wish to spend another night in the open.

So, when I'd done with the horse, I left. I took the ferry road directly, for I was anxious to get there. No longer believing I would be followed, I hastened along my way.

{ 19 }

Testimony of Nathaniel Hill,
continued

As I had planned and hoped, the boy went directly toward the westward ferry road, paying no heed to whether I observed him. Of course I did just that. Taking care, I followed as soon as it was prudent, staying back without losing sight of him.

Did I not have every reason to be pleased with myself? My methods, my care, my deliberate ease, all were proving justified. And I beg you to note how I proceeded; there were no threats, no violence. All my efforts were bent toward a peaceful resolution. Nor did I in any way break the law.

I watched the boy skirt past the ferryman's hut and continue west. I followed, pausing only to see if the ferryman was about, unsure whether to allow myself to be seen. But he was nowhere in sight, and I passed on without being hailed.

The day was dull and growing duller. The area I

entered, a forest place, was quite dark, and for a few moments I lost sight of the boy. But by pushing forward I caught a glimpse of him and knew that all was well.

Then I lost him again. I pressed forward along the trail for some time before I was sure he was no longer in front of me. Stopping, I attempted to listen for his footsteps, but the place was too full of noise and I could not detect a thing. I continued on until I became convinced that I had gone past wherever he had turned.

It was as I retraced my steps that I noticed a heap of stones by the trail. They looked odd, piled as they were. When I discovered that the moss on one lay wrong side up, I knew it was some sort of marker.

I searched about for some further sign, some indication of the path by which the boy had gone, certain it began near this spot. When I found nothing I made a circle, using the rocks as my central point. Sure enough, I found a faint but unmistakable path that led up to the hill.

It was a long path and in some places steeply inclined, but I continued on it nonetheless. Soon I spied fresh heelmarks and took them to be the boy's prints on the soft earth. It convinced me I was going in the proper direction.

I had gone some way when ahead I saw a bluff of rock directly before me that seemed to bar the way. Once there I had to choose between two ways. I was

not at a loss for long, for once again I found
footprint evidence that the boy had passed along the
base of the bluff.

I went by a place where water was dripping, not
at all sure how close I was to the boy but moving
with great caution nonetheless. This was fortunate
because I was at my goal almost before I realized it.

Directly along the bluff—I was standing some
sixty feet from it—was a pile of rubble made of
stones. Above, on the overhanging bluff, was a
blackened place that indicated a fire had been lit
below that very spot.

I edged off the path and took precautions not to be
seen. Then I simply waited.

My patience was at length rewarded when I saw
the boy emerge. He was obviously looking for
something or someone—I knew not which. After a
moment he retreated behind the stone barricade.

I was certain I had found the girl's hiding place.
But not knowing who the boy was looking for—it
might not have been the girl, for all I knew—I
turned as quietly as I could and found my way
down the hill. From there I proceeded to Easton and
Mr. Clagget, the constable, hoping to reach him
before the rain began to fall.

As I went I touched my inner pocket to make sure
that the document I needed—the one that proved
Elizabeth Mawes a runaway felon—was still there.
Placing it on my person was a small precaution I had
taken, for I had been fearful that the boy might

come across it and take it away. And, of course, having it with me now would save me time. As I have said, I am a most efficient man.

{ 20 }

Testimony of George Clagget,
continued

Mr. Nathaniel Hill returned to my office in the early evening two days after his first visit. It was already dark, and the air was thick with intimations of rain, which, as events proved, materialized within a few hours.

Once we were settled within the privacy of my chambers, he informed me that he had positively identified the location of the runaway girl, Elizabeth Mawes. Further, he informed me that she was being cared for by a boy not normally residing in Easton, that the location of the hiding place was a singular dwelling—he knew not how other to define it—and that he suspected the woman known as Mad Moll lived there.

I inquired of him whether he was certain of his information.

"As certain as I can be," he swore.

I informed him that to my previous knowledge no one had been able to discover that unfortunate woman's place of abode.

"They haven't looked very hard," he told me with evident satisfaction. "I didn't find it difficult to discover."

I asked him what the woman's relationship to the girl might be, but to this question he had no answer. Yet he was willing to swear that she was harboring the girl. I then asked him, as I am required to do by law, if he wished to bring a charge against Mad Moll.

"Certainly not," he said. "I'm interested only in the girl."

I further inquired whether he wished to bring a charge against the boy, for by Mr. Hill's oath, the boy was also shielding the girl from justice and thus unlawfully abetting her in her escape. To this question he gave a little consideration.

"I suspect," he said after a moment, "that he too is a runaway. But I have no proof of it, and I may be wrong. I was instructed only to pursue the girl."

With these questions concluded to my satisfaction, I then asked what he desired of me.

"I must ask for authority to claim the girl, as well as ask for your assistance in securing her person."

I told him both requests were reasonable if he had proof that he had a legal claim on the girl. Quickly he brought forth a document from his pocket. A careful study of said document informed me that indeed, one Elizabeth Mawes, convicted felon, branded on the thumb in His Majesty's court in England, was bound in labor to one John Tolivar, Esquire, Jersey Colony. The document was in order and bore the proper seals and signatures. I had no reason to doubt it for what it was, and indeed it did prove true. In short, I was obliged to tell him that his evidence was acceptable.

"Good," he said, taking back the paper. "I'll return in the morning. The boy will be with me. Be advised that he does not, and will not, know who I am or what I intend to do. I must ask you to detain him here while we fetch the girl."

As I was at some loss as to how this might be done, he suggested that I lock the boy in my rooms for a short time against our return. He said it was the most humane thing to do, assuring me that the boy was docile and stood in awe and fear of him. "I took my pains to make sure of that," he said.

Somewhat unhappily, I agreed to his suggestion. Beyond this—and perhaps it was something in his tone that made me say it—I told Mr. Hill I would not allow him to be armed. There was no need for arms, I said, and I wished to see no misadventure by their use. He bridled at this, and made some unpleasant suggestions, but I stood strong and he finally agreed.

Having come to this understanding, we further

agreed that he would wait upon me early the following morning. We set the hour, and I bade him a good evening. He was generous in his appreciation, apologized for his bit of temper, and left.

It had already started to rain.

{ 21 }

Testimony of Robert Linnly,
continued

I went directly to the hill, for I wanted to reach the cave room before the dark and the rain descended.

When I arrived at the old woman's place, I was surprised to see that she had gone. Instantly, I looked toward the bed, and to my great relief, Bet was still there.

I went and stood over her. She looked not greatly different, though her face seemed thinner. There was the same look of sickness on her skin, which was a waxy yellow. And when I touched my hand to her cheek, it felt hot. She still slept.

I sat there for a while, looking about me, wondering where the woman had gone and when she would return. The fire was smoldering, eyeing me with winking chunks of glowing wood. I threw some bits of wood on it and watched it grow.

I went outside the cave in search of the woman,

but I saw nothing of her. Nor did I see anything to suggest where she might have gone. I turned about and returned to Bet.

"Bet," I whispered. "Can you hear me?"

That time, her eyes quivered. But still she gave me no answer.

I tried again. "It's me, Bet. Robert."

She opened her eyes then, staring upward till I repeated my words. Then, turning slightly, she looked at me, or at least in my direction. Her eyes were dull and only half opened, but I believe she knew me. She said nothing.

"Are you feeling any better?" I whispered. "Does your arm hurt much?"

"Yes," she said at last. She spoke in a voice so low that I had to lean forward to understand her words.

"You've been sick," I told her, glad that she at least could talk. "But you're getting better, I can see that," I said, not truly believing it.

"Where are we?" she wanted to know.

"An old woman took us here," I answered, looking around to see if the woman had returned, and glad that she had not. "I don't know who she is, but she has been kind to you. And Bet," I began, grasping her hand, "I've got work, Bet, and will get money. The mare is gone, though. She slipped in the river, skinned her knee, and ran away. I tried to catch her but I couldn't."

Bet had closed her eyes again, and she said nothing.

I considered telling her about Mr. Hill but I thought it would only trouble her, and so I did not mention him. Instead I said, "Bet, all you have to do is get well. No one shall ever bother us again."

She nodded her head slightly.

"Are you going to sleep again?" I asked, disappointed.

She made a small movement, which I took to be yes. "I'm tired," she whispered. "I'm tired all the time."

"Are you hungry?" I asked. But once more she had fallen asleep.

For a long time I kept my place near her, but at last I went to the front of the room and stood there looking out over the darkling woods. It had grown very dim. The air was thick, and in the distance I heard the approach of thunder. And still I saw no sign of the woman.

Feeling anxious, I sat on the ground wishing the rain would start and clear the air. As I watched I saw the tips of trees begin to tremble. I knew the rain would not be long in coming.

I was hungry—I had not eaten since the morning—and worried about Elizabeth. I looked about for food but found nothing except some dried berries. They tasted terrible, and I had to spit them out.

Though I had no wish to fall asleep, I grew tired and lay down on the ground not far from Bet. Thunder drew closer. I closed my eyes.

When I awoke it was completely dark. The first I heard was a steady beat of rain sounding like many men running through the woods, their feet padded by the duff. Then, mixed with the beat of the rain, I heard a low, whispering, singing voice.

I sat up.

Between me and the low-burning fire sat the woman, her black shape darker than the dark, as though the night was compressed in her. She sat with her knees drawn up and held in her arms; her head was bowed on her breast. She was rocking back and forth, singing. I listened to her song, wanting to hear the words. It took a while for me to understand them, but what she sang was this:

> *"The way of my world*
> *Is goverened by wind*
> *The crying, the darkness and rain.*
>
> *Windblown I've come*
> *And windblown I'll go*
> *To the darkness from whence I came*
> *To the rain which never goes 'way.*
>
> *Yes, crying I've come*
> *And crying I'll pass away."*

Over and over she sang her song until I could no longer tell her voice from the running of the rain.

Again I slept.

Testimony of Robert Linnly,
continued

It was still raining the next morning. Water dripped down over the entryway,
making a large puddle. Such was the general
grayness that the walls of the place and the outside
air seemed one and the same.

The first thing I did when I awoke was to look at
Bet. She lay quiet and unmoving. I thought her face
even yellower than before, but decided it was only
the light.

The woman was asleep too, but on the ground
near the fire, which had now burned very low. In
her old clothes she looked like a bundle of rags.
Beside her lay bits of bark. She must have been
seeking medicine for Elizabeth.

I went to the mouth of the cave and stood there,
staring out. The rain, falling constantly if not hard,
was the only sound I could hear. Every surface
glistened, and the air, filled with a kind of mist,

seemed soft enough to melt. The chilly dampness made me shiver.

After taking another look at Bet, and then at the woman asleep on the floor, I ran out along the bluff wall. I tried to keep myself as close to the wall as possible. There was water everywhere, but because the bluff hung over me, it provided some shelter. Even so, before I reached the turning I was thoroughly wet and cold. I hoped there would be a fire at the inn.

When I reached the inn, I went first to the stable. It was steamy and warm. I fed Mr. Hill's horse and brought new water.

In the main building the big taproom was empty and a fine fire was burning. The heat was wonderfully soothing, and the chill I had worn like a coat began to fall from me.

The tapman entered, greeted me cheerily, and bade me stay where I was. I turned myself about before the fireplace, trying to dry on all sides, like a piece of mutton on a spit.

The tapman kindly offered me some hot cider. "Bit of rum in it," he warned. "That's to dry your toes."

I drank it and felt it did me much good.

"I think I heard your master moving about upstairs," the tapman told me after a while.

I drained the last of the cider, then went to Mr. Hill's door. His boots had been placed outside, so I took them and brought them down before the fire to clean. As I was doing this Mr. Hill himself came down.

"Ah, you're here," he greeted me. "I was wondering if you'd come. It looks a bad day."

He went to the window and looked out at the rain. Though it had lessened somewhat, it still fell at a steady pace.

"I shouldn't think anyone would move about in that, do you?" he asked me.

"No, sir."

"Did you ask your relation if I might come to talk?" he inquired matter-of-factly, his face still turned from me.

The question took me by surprise, for I had forgotten about his request. "I did, sir," I managed awkwardly. "But he hardly expects you to come on a day like this." Right then I resolved that as soon as possible I must quit Mr. Hill.

"Quite right," Mr. Hill agreed, turning to look at me. "Quite right. It would be the last thing he'd expect. Have you had your breakfast?"

"Something to drink."

"Then sit down with me," he ordered, and after a few words with the tapman, he sat down at the table.

I continued to polish his boots, aware that he was looking steadily at me. When the food was brought, he called me over and I ate along with him.

The meal done, he ordered me to clear away the dishes, which I did, secreting some bread in my pocket for Bet. On my return from the kitchen I found him once more at the window, hands behind his back, staring at the rain. I waited impatiently to see what he would say or do, hoping he would release me so that I could return to Bet. I was that determined not to work any longer for Mr. Hill.

"You're right," he finally said. "It won't do any good to go out today. I'll see nothing and only get wet for my effort. We'll be like other folk and go nowhere at all."

I experienced a great swell of relief.

"Only," he continued, "I shall be wanting to visit a man this morning with whom I have business. Do you by chance know a Mr. Clagget?"

"No, sir," I replied, "I don't."

"It doesn't matter," said Mr. Hill with a shrug. "As soon as you finish those boots, we'll go. One wants to look one's best at business. I'll need you to come and mind my horse, but when my affair with Mr. Clagget is done, you'll be free to go."

Greatly pleased by his decision, I was only too happy to hasten my tasks. As soon as I had done his boots I presented them for his inspection. He looked them over carefully, pronounced them in perfect order, and put them on.

"Now," he said, "fetch the horse."

"The saddlebags, sir?" I asked.

He looked at me. "No," he said. "I've no need for them. No need at all. I've done with hunting."

I ran out to the stable, saddled his horse, and

brought her around to the front of the inn. Mr. Hill mounted and pulled me up behind him. As we moved down the muddy market street, I was cheered by the thought of soon being free.

{ 23 }

Testimony of George Clagget,
continued

Mr. Hill returned in the morning.
The hour was early, and it was yet raining. My wife, Mrs. Clagget, admitted the man and the boy who accompanied him, bringing them directly to my room. I had not expected Mr. Hill so early, but I greeted him cordially just the same.

When he entered, the boy hung back. Mr. Hill urged him forward, and he came into the room.

He was a young boy, poorly dressed, and at the moment rather the worse for the rain. It was perfectly clear that he had no understanding of what was about to occur.

As soon as the boy was in the room, Mr. Hill nodded to me. Taking my key from my pocket, I closed the door and locked it. The boy looked at me when I did this, but he said and did nothing.

Having secured the door, I went around to my desk. I had laid out the necessary forms, waiting only for the entry of names and signatures.

I began by asking Mr. Hill if everything was in proper order.

"I believe so," he replied, quite clearly in the best of spirits.

Taking up my quill, I inquired after the girl's name. As I did so, the boy turned about and looked at me with great surprise.

"Elizabeth Mawes," pronounced Mr. Hill.

"Are you prepared," I asked him, "to swear that said girl, a bonded servant, branded felon, and transported person from England to His Majesty's colonies, owned by Mr. John Tolivar, Esquire, of Trenton, Jersey Colony, is close at hand?"

The boy was now staring wildly at me. All the same, I continued by asking Mr. Hill if he could produce proof of his claim to the said girl, Elizabeth Mawes.

"I can," he said. So saying, he produced the document from his vest. "Here is the contract for her labor," he said, handing it to me.

I had already seen this document and testified to its correctness, and thus I merely noted that it was the same and returned it to him.

"Do you," I went on, "know where said girl is presently hiding?"

"I do," he swore.

At these words, the boy, who had seemed stupefied and incapable of any action whatsoever, suddenly leaped to the door, gripped the handle, and attempted to pull it open. Of course he found it locked and unmovable.

Meanwhile, I entered the relevant material onto my own papers and informed Mr. Hill that I was signing for the retention and return of the girl, the said Elizabeth Mawes. I signed my document, scattered the blotting sand, and handed the paper to him. He approved it at a glance and returned it to me.

In short, everything was done in complete and perfect order.

I then required Mr. Hill to pay the normal fee of two shillings, which he did, making the remark that it was a fair price and the same wage he owed the boy for his work. "I apologize for the weather," he added, "but there is no help for it."

I thanked him for his thoughtful words, merely telling him that I trusted I knew my duty, no matter how discomforting it might be.

I then addressed the boy in as solemn a manner as I could. I informed him that a serious charge had been leveled at him, and that had it not been for the kindness of Mr. Hill, he would have been arrested. Further, I told him that he was being detained in my house by the full order and weight of the law which I, George Clagget, Esquire, represented. Further, I begged to inform him that he was bound to make no effort to counter my expressed orders to remain, and that to act otherwise would be to engage the displeasure of myself.

Having so informed him, I was careful to ask Mr. Hill if the boy understood what I had said.

Mr. Hill took it upon himself to say that it took a fool to know a fool and that he must understand.

As I unlocked the door the boy made yet another attempt, a violent attempt, to flee. But Mr. Hill caught him up and forcibly restrained him by thrusting him cleanly to the floor.

Taking the opportunity of the moment, we both stepped through the door. I made sure to lock it again from the other side. We then proceeded to our horses, after which Mr. Hill began to lead the way to the place where the girl was hiding.

Sir, may I take the liberty to point out that I acted in complete accordance with the law.

{ 24 }

Testimony of Robert Linnly,
continued

They shut the door on me, locked it, and left. I was unable to do a thing save stand in the middle of the room, stunned at what had happened. I could not believe what had been done. I had been fooled, toyed with, made to betray Bet!

I did not remain motionless for long. I understood all too well what they were doing and where they were going. It was perfectly clear from what had been said that they knew exactly where Elizabeth was.

I flung myself at the door repeatedly, trying to pull it open, but to no avail. I shouted, cried, and screamed. No one came. I tried to smash the door with my hands. That, too, was useless.

I searched for some way, any way, to get out. Running to the window, I tried to pull it open, but it gave way no more than the door. Then I went to Mr. Clagget's desk, found an open drawer, and there discovered a knife. I tried to force open the window with it, but the knife blade snapped in two.

Then, hardly thinking what I was doing, I picked up a chair and smashed it against the window, so desperate was I to get out. The small glass panes broke away and the wood ribs splintered. Not caring how much noise I made, I swung and swung again.

I soon heard a woman's voice from behind the door. She was shouting at me, telling me to stop what I was doing. The knowledge that someone was closeby only made me smash at the window even more. Soon there was nothing left—glass and pieces of wood were everywhere.

I climbed up on the sill, crawled out, and let myself drop on the soft wet ground. As I picked myself up I could hear the woman shouting to her neighbors to come and help her.

I raced out to the main street only to see people running toward the building from which I had just escaped. Frantically, I ran the other way, behind other houses. The people I saw there did not yet know the cause for alarm and paid me no heed.

I swung around the few houses only to return to the main street some way farther down. It was still raining, and thus few people were about. No doubt that is what saved me from being caught.

At first I wasn't sure what I could do. I merely raced down the length of the road. But as soon as I saw the inn, I formed a plan. I raced into the inn, paying no heed to the tapman's friendly call.

Bursting into Mr. Hill's room, I went at once to his saddlebags and looked into them. The double-barreled pistol was still there. I took up the bags, with the gun inside, and ran out of the building and to the stable.

Mr. Hill had taken his own horse, but in my fear I did not care whose horse I took. I untied a mare, backed her, and led her outside. There I clammered on her back, throwing the saddlebags before me. One kick and we were out on the road, though as I went I heard the tapman shout to me.

I paid no heed. I beat the horse and made it gallop down the road, leaving the shouts quickly behind.

Down the ferry road we went, mud and rain flying about me. Ever more desperate, I tried to make the horse go still faster. Past the ferryman's house we sped until we reached the narrower path where the horse slowed. I pressed her until we reached the stone marking, where I found Mr. Hill's and Mr. Clagget's horses tied to a tree.

I leaped off the mare, pulling the saddlebags with me, and not even caring if the horse was tied, I ran up the hill. The rain was still falling; soaking bushes and branches of trees whipped at me and held me back.

At the top of the hill, up against the bluff, I stopped, trying to catch my breath. I leaned against the shelter of the stone wall, opened a saddlebag, and took out the pistol, making sure it was still loaded.

My fingers shook, but I kept the gun safe from the rain within the bag as I drew back the flints. Then, still using the bag to keep the pistol dry, I began to run along the path.

As I approached the woman's place I heard a scream so high and piercing that it made me stop. Again and again it came.

Frantic, I leaped forward to the walls of the cave room, ran around it, and stood in the entrance.

Mr. Clagget and Mr. Hill were standing in the middle of the area. Between them and where Bet lay was the woman. Her hair was wild and her mouth was open so wide that I could see the redness of her tongue. In her hand she held a branch of wood that was burning at the end.

"Come, my good woman," Mr. Clagget was saying. "We must have her. She's nothing to do with you. We mean you no harm. It's the girl we want. We represent the law and are obliged to uphold it."

The woman only screamed at them, a wordless scream of rage from deep within her throat. She swung the burning stick wildly in a great circle, so they dared not come closer. Then she began cursing at them, her eyes aflame with anger. "She's my daughter!" she shouted. "You'll not take my daughter! She's mine! Go away!"

Mr. Clagget kept trying to draw closer, but at every step he took she swung the stick, and he was forced to back away. Meanwhile Mr. Hill was trying to edge himself around so that he might gain an advantage from the other side.

When I realized what was happening, I pulled the pistol from the bag and shouted, "Bet, get up! You must get up!"

My shouting startled the two men, causing them to turn about and face me. I stood there with Mr. Hill's pistol in hand, the flints cocked.

"Mr. Hill!" cried Mr. Clagget, who suddenly became frightened for himself. "Mr. Hill! You must do something. This must not happen!"

Mr. Hill swore an oath and began to come directly at me, his hand extended. "Give me that gun, boy. Do you hear me? Give it to me!"

"Leave her alone!" I cried. "Leave her alone!" With both my hands on the pistol, I leveled the gun directly at him. He stopped, perplexed.

"I mean her no harm," he said to me, advancing yet another step. "No harm at all."

"Don't move!" I shouted in warning. "Leave her be!"

It was Mr. Clagget who gave way first. "For God's sake, man," he cried to Mr. Hill. "The boy will shoot. Don't tempt him, man, don't do it!"

Mr. Hill stood motionless, unsure what to do. But as he stood there the woman began to act. Dropping her burning stick on the ground, she ran and snatched Elizabeth up from where she lay. Carrying her bodily, she burst between the two men, ran past me out into the rain and down the hill.

"Woman!" cried Mr. Clagget. "You must not do that!"

With the woman and Elizabeth now behind me, I began to back out through the entrance, the pistol still pointed at Mr. Hill. Suddenly he made a lunge at me, his face showing great rage.

Startled, I gripped the pistol and pulled one of the triggers. In the closeness of the place the explosion was huge, roaring in my ears, blinding my eyes. Even as it went off, the pistol tore itself from my grasp and fell to the ground. Though I could not see what had happened, I heard a sharp cry of "Damn!"

Not waiting to see what I had done, or even trying to retrieve the gun, I spun about and ran in search of Bet. I saw the woman struggling through the woods below, Bet in her arms.

I leaped after them, slipping and stumbling on the sodden earth and leaves, not daring to look back to see if the men were following.

I caught up with the woman soon enough. The rain had soaked her through, matting her hair and clothing so that she seemed to have shrunk, becoming almost as small as Bet, whom she still carried in her arms. Hardly knowing I was there, she labored desperately on, sucking in great gulps and sobs of breath. Mixed in were words, gasping words that went beyond my understanding.

I looked back. Mr. Hill had bounded after us and was close behind. There was no time to do anything. Even as I saw him, he raised his right arm, the pistol in his hand.

"*Bet!*" I cried.

The report of the gun came upon that instant.

The woman, who had never ceased running, let out a low grunt, tripped, and fell. Elizabeth, flung upon the ground, began to roll wildly down the hill—arms, legs, and hair a windmill of horrible confusion.

I flung myself after her to stop her fall, my body shielding hers. So we lay until Mr. Hill came.

"Get up!" he ordered. Grabbing me by the back of my neck, he yanked me away, then knelt by Bet, his hand on her.

I did not care anymore, for I already knew that Bet was dead.

{25}

Testimony of George Clagget,
concluded

Though I tried to prevent the tragedy, there was nothing, as any fair-minded person can see, that I could have done.

The woman Mad Moll was killed by Mr. Hill, who had recovered his pistol. Since the woman was unlawfully aiding and abetting the escape of a felon, there was no charge I could place against him.

As for Elizabeth Mawes, how she died could not be determined. She might have been dead when first we discovered her in the cave. We subsequently learned that she had been gravely ill. On the other hand, she might have died as a result of her fall when the woman dropped her. In the end it made no difference; she was dead.

The boy had wounded Mr. Hill, but that gentleman refused to swear a complaint against him, saying that there was nothing in it for him. Mr. Hill's anger was directed against Mr. Tolivar, the man on whose mission he had come. Indeed, after the encounter Mr. Hill insisted on leaving for Trenton at once, asking of me no more than a signed statement saying that he had caught the girl. He left saying that it was as pretty a five pounds as he had ever won.

As for the boy, at the time I had no positive proof of who he was. And when Mr. Grey, the tapman at the inn, heard what had happened, he offered to take responsibility for the boy. When word later came that the boy was a runaway, this same Mr. Grey arranged to buy his contract from Mr. Toliver. The boy thus remains in Easton with a new master. Although why anyone would want such a violent creature I cannot say.

One curious incident remains to tell. The boy insisted on burying both the girl and the woman. I beg to state that it was not a proper burial. Indeed, rather hysterically the boy actually demanded that the deceased be buried where they fell on the hill, close together, as if they were mother and daughter.

He was assisted in this by the tapman from the inn, Mr. Grey. That same man informed me that the boy refused to leave the site of the incident and remained in the woods until the rain had ceased and until beams of sunlight broke through the trees. The place where one of these beams touched the earth was the spot the boy chose for their graves.

Not, I am the first to admit, a Christian burial. When this unfortunate burial was completed—

so Mr. Grey told me—the boy looked up toward this ray of light saying not a thing. After a long time, he suddenly shouted, "Hold them! Hold them kindly!"

What these odd words meant no one understood.

Avi a librarian at Trenton State College, is also a teacher of children's literature and often performs readings of his books in schools and libraries. His previously published books, including *Captain Grey*, "a robust adventure with a neat twist" (*The New York Times Book Review*), *Night Journeys*, and two successive runners-up for the Mystery Writers of America Award, *No More Magic* and *Emily Upham's Revenge* have established him as a gifted writer of suspense and adventure for young readers.

Avi lives in New Hope, Pennsylvania, with his wife Joan, a weaver, and their two teen-aged sons.